the
prom
queen

Books by Melody Carlson

Devotions for Real Life

Double Take

Just Another Girl

Anything but Normal

Never Been Kissed

Allison O'Brian on Her Own—Volume 1

Allison O'Brian on Her Own—Volume 2

LIFE AT KINGSTON HIGH

The Jerk Magnet

The Best Friend

The Prom Queen

Life at Kingston High

the
prom
queen

Melody Carlson

Revell

a division of Baker Publishing Group
Grand Rapids, Michigan

© 2013 by Melody Carlson

Published by Revell
a division of Baker Publishing Group
P.O. Box 6287, Grand Rapids, MI 49516-6287
www.revellbooks.com

Printed in the United States of America

Library of Congress Cataloging-in-Publication Data
Carlson, Melody.
    The prom queen : a novel / Melody Carlson.
        pages cm. — (Life at Kingston High)
    Summary: "Life gets more and more complicated for a high school girl who decides to do whatever it takes to be elected as prom queen"—Provided by publisher.
    ISBN 978-0-8007-1961-6 (pbk.)
    1. Proms—Fiction. 2. Dating (Social customs)—Fiction. 3. High schools—Fiction. 4. Schools—Fiction. 5. Christian life—Fiction.] I. Title.
PZ7.C216637Pu 2013
[Fic]—dc23   2012032498

Scripture quotations are from the New Century Version®. Copyright © 1987, 1988, 1991 by Word Publishing, a division of Thomas Nelson, Inc. Used by permission. All rights reserved.

13 14 15 16 17 18 19   7 6 5 4 3 2 1

one

Megan Bernard didn't usually tune in to watch television preachers. But when she announced she was too ill to attend church, Mom wasn't buying.

"You don't look sick to me." She barely touched Megan's forehead, then gave her an ultimatum. "If you can't make it to church, you can at least watch *Shower of Power* on television. It starts at ten o'clock. If you hurry you won't miss a thing."

Megan obediently went down to the basement and turned on the television. As she squirmed into Mom's hot pink Snuggie blanket, she wondered why her mother wanted her to watch an infomercial about bath products. However, it turned out to be a preacher dude called Pastor Robbie Martin, and although Megan was tempted to change channels on him, she continued to watch. Partly because Pastor Robbie wasn't too hard on the eyes and partly because she suspected Mom might give her a pop quiz when she got home.

At the beginning of the show, Megan thought this guy's

sermon was a bunch of hooey, but the more she listened, the more it made sense. Or else her fever was messing with her head and she was becoming delusional.

"Name it and claim it!" he proclaimed with earnest-looking blue eyes. "Don't be afraid to dream big, dear friends! If you can picture what you desire in your mind and if you can feel it your heart, it *will* become yours. I am a living testimony of this truth!"

Megan pulled out a fresh tissue and loudly blew her nose as she watched Pastor Robbie with growing interest. What if what he said was really true?

"Believe it and receive it!" Pastor Robbie's bright Colgate smile was dazzling and about three feet wide on their big flat-screen television. "And I promise you, dear friend, you *will be* showered with power! Believe and receive!"

An upbeat gospel song began to play, and Pastor Robbie's deeply tanned face slowly faded out. Megan sighed as she turned off the TV with the remote. As she sat there, still wrapped in her mom's frowsy Snuggie, she seriously considered what she'd just heard. What if it were really true? What if she could use positive thinking to get what she wanted? What if she could change her seriously lackluster life?

She thought about how her senior year had gone so far, and two words came to mind: dismal and disappointing. It was nothing like she'd expected. She'd had such high hopes last summer. Senior year was going to be significant and memorable. But so far she would rather just forget it. The school year was more than half over, and she felt helpless to change direction. Like she was stuck in a rut.

Megan pulled out another tissue and wiped her nose carefully this time since it was feeling a little raw and sore now. Kind of like how she felt inside, because something was definitely hurting. Was it Pastor Robbie's words that had touched that tender place? Or was this head cold just making her blow things out of proportion? She couldn't deny that she'd felt a smidgen of hope at his optimistic words. She almost believed she could change the course of her life, yet at the same time she felt confused and clueless.

"What if it is true?" she mused out loud. "Except that it sounds too good to be true." She sighed. "I wish it was true—"

"Hey, what're you doing down here? Who are you talking to?" Megan's older sister Belinda tromped down the stairs with a surprised expression.

"No one." Megan pushed up the sleeves of the Snuggie. "What're you doing here? I thought you were on your way back to college."

"And I thought you'd still be at church." Belinda frowned. "Hey, why are you home anyway?"

Megan explained about her cold. "Mom and Arianna went without me." She pointed the remote at the television. "But Mom made me watch *Shower of Power*."

Belinda laughed. "You mean that cheesy televangelist who's always saying, 'Believe it and receive it'?"

Megan nodded. "You've seen him?"

"Mom made me watch him when I was here during the holidays. She thinks that guy practically walks on water." Belinda rolled her eyes. "But really, he's just a religious dork."

To Megan's surprise, she felt like defending Pastor Robbie. Instead she just shrugged, pulling her knees up into the Snuggie. "So . . . why aren't you on your way back to school already?" Belinda had been home for the weekend, and her campus was a couple hours away.

"We were just heading out when I remembered something I forgot." Belinda went over to a closet that was supposed to be reserved for guests but was mostly used for overflow storage for the girls. With four females in the household, closet space was always at a premium. "There's this big dance in a couple of weeks, and I hoped I might find something in here that I can rework into a cocktail dress." Belinda started to pull out formals, tossing them onto the sofa until Megan was nearly buried in tulle and satin and lace.

"Remember this one?" Belinda held up a pale pink number with a wistful smile. "It's a Theia gown."

Megan pushed a scratchy red dress away from her face as she peered up at the dress. "Was that from prom?"

"Not *just* prom." Belinda held the dress close to her with a dreamy look. "This dress is from when I was crowned *Kingston High Prom Queen*." She began to dance and twirl her way around the room now. "What a night, oh, what a night!" She laughed, then tossed the dress onto the growing pile around Megan. "I'd offer it to you to use if I thought there was any chance you'd ever be elected prom queen—or fit into it." She laughed, then returned to pillaging the closet.

Megan was reminded of all the reasons she hadn't missed her older sister too much during the past months. Belinda could be sweet at times, but when she was in a bad mood, watch out! Still, Megan knew better than to react.

"Sorry, sis. I shouldn't have said that." Belinda held up a black gown. "It's not fair to tease someone about something they can't help. It's kind of like kicking a puppy."

Megan frowned. "What can't I help?"

Belinda tossed the black dress down. "You know, never competing for prom queen. It's not your fault you can't—"

"What's that supposed to mean?" Megan's hurt feelings were replaced with anger now.

"You know what it means. And it's okay, really. Not everyone can be prom queen. It's kind of like a calling . . . or a gift. A gift that only a few lucky girls can handle." She laughed like she thought this was clever.

"I could be prom queen if I wanted."

Belinda laughed even louder now. "Yeah, right!"

Megan stood. Still wearing Mom's hot pink Snuggie, she went over to where Belinda was holding up a red sequined dress. "It's just that I don't want to," Megan declared.

Belinda tossed her a sugar-coated sympathy nod. "Yeah, sure, I understand, sweetie."

"I don't!" Megan glared at her. "I have absolutely no interest in being prom queen. I think it's totally ridiculous."

"It's okay, Meggie. That's what all the girls say—the girls who know they don't have a chance. It's just a case of sour grapes . . . It's easier that way. I understand."

Megan attempted to blow angry air through her stuffy nostrils, but it sounded more like a sneeze. "I *could* be prom queen, Belinda! That is, if I wanted it bad enough. It's just that I don't."

Belinda firmly shook her head. "Wanting it isn't enough, Megan. You have to be *popular* to be prom queen."

"I am popular." Megan frowned and rethought this. "Anyway, I used to be popular."

"Middle school doesn't count, sis." Belinda reached over

and patted Megan's head in a placating way. Then she jerked her hand back and made a disgusted expression. "Eeeuw! Someone needs a good shampoo."

"I'm sick!" Megan spewed back at her.

"Then get away from me." Belinda held her hands up like a blockade. "I don't want your sick germs."

Stepping back, Megan tripped on the hem of the Snuggie, then tumbled backward, landing in the pile of formals, which sent Belinda into new spasms of laughter. But at least she stepped over and offered a hand.

"Poor Meggie," Belinda said as she pulled Megan up. "I know it can't be easy being you. I'm sorry."

Megan flopped back onto the dress-splattered sofa and groaned. "And it's so easy being you?"

Belinda gave her a somber look. "The truth is, it's not nearly as easy as it used to be. You know, Meggie, sometimes I wish I was still back in high school. Life was so much easier then."

"You've got to be kidding." Megan felt her hopes being dashed again. She'd been looking forward to going to college next year, telling herself that it would be better than this year. "You wish you were still in high school?"

"At least I was *somebody* in high school." Belinda pressed her lips together as she sat down. "The truth is . . . I some-times feel completely lost in college."

Megan tried not to look too surprised, but she was shocked. She'd never heard her "perfect" older sister confess to any sort of hardship in any part of her life. To Megan, Belinda's life was just one great big walk in the park. The worst thing she'd ever witnessed going wrong for Belinda was her getting a small zit before a big date. Then she'd cleverly conceal it with one of her magical beauty products. Even when Alex Bronson "broke her heart," Belinda managed to find a new and improved boyfriend the very next day.

"Take it from me, you really should make the most of your last year of high school." Belinda picked up a previously discarded lacy, cream-colored dress from the floor, looking at it more carefully. "Because once it's gone, it's gone. You can't go back and do it all over again." She made a little smile. "Although I still have high school dreams occasionally. Very sweet."

"I dream about getting *out* of high school," Megan admitted.

Belinda just shook her head. "Too bad for you." She held up the cream dress. "What about this for the Sweetheart's Ball? If I shortened it and added a wide red belt and matching heels? Ya think?"

Megan nodded. "Yeah, that'd probably look great."

"Thanks, sis." Belinda smiled. "I really do wish you had what it takes to be prom queen, sweetie. Seriously, I'd do anything to help you with a campaign. It would be very cool to keep the crown in the family. But trust me, some battles are best left unfought. Really, I do understand."

Megan forced a smile. "Yeah . . ."

"Gotta go. Celeste is waiting. Tell Mom and Ari bye for me, okay?"

Megan watched as Belinda skipped up the stairs with the cream dress flying behind her like a cape—like she was Supergirl. Maybe she was. Megan peeled off the fuzzy Snuggie, which felt way too warm now. Then she started picking up the dresses Belinda had left strewn about. But instead of hanging them up, Megan simply shoved them into the already crowded closet. Until she came to the last one, the pale pink prom queen formal.

Fingering the silky fabric, she studied the delicately stitched bodice with embroidery and tiny glass beads. Very princess-like. Maybe it wasn't her style exactly, but she wondered what it would feel like to wear something this pretty. Carrying it over to the bathroom, she held it up in front of the mirror above the sink, expecting to see a princess. But when she saw her reflection, she cringed in dismay.

With her dull and greasy brown hair, a cluster of zits that strangely resembled Orion's Belt on her chin, pale chapped lips, and bloodshot eyes in a washed-out shade of blue, she knew her sister was absolutely right—Megan was definitely not prom queen material. Not now, not a few weeks from now, not ever!

"See yourself as the person you want to be!" Pastor Robbie's enthusiastic words echoed in her mind. "Believe you can and *you can*. You can do anything you put your mind to—just put your mind to it and do it!"

Megan thought hard about that. What if Pastor Robbie was right? What if she was simply the victim of her own negative thinking? He'd talked a lot about the wall of rejection. What if she'd created that big nasty wall around herself and it was keeping the bad things in and the good things out? What if he was right?

Megan hadn't been happy with her life for a while now. But what had she done to change anything? Most of the time she acted like she didn't care. The problem was, she did care. She didn't like feeling like a loser. What if she took Pastor

Robbie's advice and changed her thinking, and what if that really did change her life? What was stopping her? What if it was simply her own doubt and disbelief keeping her from having all the things she deserved? Anyway, how would she know if she didn't at least try?

In that very instant, Megan decided it was time to change the course of her life. She closed her eyes and took in several slow, deep breaths, and standing right there in the basement bathroom, she waited—as if she expected something amazing to happen. When nothing did, she began to replay some of Pastor Robbie's words, and she attempted to erase the defeated image she'd just seen in the badly lit bathroom mirror. She tried to envision herself differently. For inspiration, she thought about her sister. She imagined herself in the same way she saw Belinda—beautiful, confident, upbeat, lively, fun, popular, stylish.

Yet Megan knew it was impossible. She could *never* be like that—it just wasn't how she was made. She might as well give up right now and accept her life for what it was—boring, ordinary, dreary, blah. And she was ready to do just that, except that Pastor Robbie's words kept coming at her, pushing her, encouraging her, telling her she could do more, be more, have more. "Don't settle for less than your very best, dear friend. Just do your best and let God do the rest!"

With eyes still tightly closed, Megan called on every fiber of her being to become her best—to do her best. In the same way she'd focus her energy on acing a test, she told herself that she *could* do this! Summoning every last bit of her mental and creative energy, she tried again to envision herself as this fairy-tale person—lovely and capable, witty and smart, pretty and popular. Suddenly something happened—something seemed to click inside of her. It felt almost like a miracle or like a scene from a movie, because she suddenly saw herself in a whole new light.

Megan pictured herself wearing a pale blue gown, sort of like Cinderella wore when she waltzed with the prince, but Megan was walking gracefully up to a spotlit stage. Wearing glistening opalescent shoes, Megan held her head high, and with every glossy hair in place, she waved at the cheering crowd of well-wishers. Everything about her radiated beauty and grace and style as she smiled humbly but prettily. As an enormous, glittering prom queen crown was placed upon her head, the applause and cheering grew louder and more enthusiastic. They loved her, they really loved her!

With a hopeful and pounding heart, Megan just stood there on the cold tile of the bathroom floor, clinging to her sister's gown. She kept her eyes tightly closed, wanting to grab onto this moment, to indelibly imprint that beautiful image into her mind, her heart, and her memory. She wanted to use all her energy to generate enough faith to really and truly believe it. She knew that in order to receive it, she needed to completely and wholeheartedly believe it. And she did! She really, truly did! It could happen. It would happen. Megan Bernard was destined to be Kingston High School's prom queen this spring—she just knew it!

two

After Megan's amazing moment of truth in the basement bathroom, she concluded that she not only needed to transform her inner self (her mind, heart, and spirit) but she also needed to renovate her exterior. And she realized she had less than two months to accomplish this feat. To be precise, she had six weeks to completely revamp her life in preparation for the crown. That was exactly forty days, and she didn't plan to waste a moment.

To this end, Megan decided to make herself a schedule. Mom had always been a firm believer in the power of the schedule. Up until the BD (big divorce) three years ago, their refrigerator had always been covered by an enormous whiteboard schedule that Mom claimed was their family's best form of salvation, next to God. But the schedule had disappeared shortly after Dad left. The truth was, Megan still missed them both. She wasn't sure what had become of the giant whiteboard, but Dad and his new girlfriend had relocated to Seattle, where he was pursuing a new career—in an alternative rock band. Megan was still scratching her head over that one. But at least Dad still called regularly and sent money when he had it, and Megan knew that despite what Mom called his musical midlife crisis, Dad still loved his three girls.

After a couple of ditched attempts to draw out a prom queen schedule on notebook paper, Megan resorted to her computer and was forced to learn how to use the spreadsheet program. After mastering that, she did some online searching and gathered up what seemed like critical information about how to win the crown. Of course, it was too late to take up cheerleading or debate team, like one website suggested, but she still had time to start a book club or participate in a fundraiser. And according to one prom queen expert, it was never too late to become more friendly to classmates. The site claimed that the girls with the best prom queen potential knew how to befriend everyone and anyone. This took Megan a bit by surprise since she didn't recall Belinda reaching out beyond her own circle of friends. But according to Prom Queen Diva (which seemed to be the best site), Megan needed to get comfortable talking to all sorts of kids, no matter who they were. A vote, after all, was a vote!

One particular thing that she read on the Prom Queen Diva site really seemed to stand out—and it was directly aligned with what Pastor Robbie had said on *Shower of Power* this morning. This slogan impressed her so much that she decided to make it her own secret mantra: *Act as if you have already won the prom queen crown. Think of yourself as royalty, and you will become royalty.*

The more she thought about this kind of positive positioning, the more she realized that it was exactly how Belinda had always acted—her entire life. Belinda lived as if she were prom queen both before and after she was elected. This had to be the secret to her success, and Megan felt certain she could make it work for herself as well. Okay, there was a small part of Megan that questioned this—was it shallow or self-centered? But then she realized this was the "dooming voice of the naysayer," so she decided to ignore it.

By midafternoon, Megan had managed to create a rather impressive looking schedule, complete with color-coded tasks and an exhaustive "Countdown to Prom" checklist which included a shopping list, exercise regimen, beautification plan, and suggested reading list. She was just hitting Print on her computer when her mom knocked on her bedroom door.

"Are you feeling better?" Mom asked with concern.

"Yeah." Megan nodded as she caught a page from the printer and examined it for print quality. "I'm fine."

"Then why are you still in your pajamas?" Mom came over to see what Megan was working on. "And why are you holed up in your room?"

"Just working on something." She caught another page.

"Homework?"

Megan turned, gave Mom a confident prom queen smile, and began to explain in one long, run-on sentence about Pastor Robbie and the power of positive thinking and her conversation with Belinda and the power of optimism and how it was about to change her life. She paused to catch her breath and another page from her printer.

"That's wonderful, dear."

"And that is why I have decided to run for prom queen this year." Megan skimmed a page as she waited for Mom to react to her announcement.

"Oh . . . ?" Mom sounded doubtful.

"I realize I have a lot of work to do before prom," Megan admitted. "So I decided to make a schedule. You know, like you used to post on the refrigerator. I need a routine to keep me on task." She spread several pages of her schedule across her dresser for Mom to see.

"Wow, Megan, that looks . . . well, very industrious."

"You know me, Mom." Megan pushed a strand of greasy hair from her forehead. "When I finally decide to do something, I go all out."

"What's going on in here?" Arianna pushed open the bedroom door and peeked in with an impish expression.

"Go away," Megan told her.

"Be nice," Mom warned.

Megan tossed Arianna a threatening glance. It wasn't that she didn't love her little sister, but lately Arianna had turned into a total pest. It was as if she suddenly thought she was Megan's age, although she was only twelve. Even worse, Arianna had recently taken to sneaking into Megan's room and "borrowing" clothes without even bothering to ask. Then instead of returning them, she'd hide them in the bottom of the dirty clothes hamper.

"I thought you were sick." Arianna peered suspiciously at her.

"Thanks for your concern, but I'm fine now."

"What are you guys doing in here?" Arianna pointed to a

page of schedule falling onto the floor beneath the
"What's that?"

"Megan is . . . well, she is considering a campaign for prom queen." Mom said this hesitantly, almost as if she was questioning Megan's sanity.

"Prom queen?" Arianna stared at Megan with incredulous eyes. "You gotta be kidding." Now she started to laugh loudly.

"See!" Megan pointed a finger at her sister. "You are exactly what I *don't* need."

"What you do need is a reality check." Arianna wrinkled her nose. "And a bath!"

Megan picked up a ball cap and threw it at Arianna. "Get out of here, brat!"

"Girls!" Mom frowned. "No fighting."

"Then tell Arianna to stop aggravating me."

"I'm just trying to help you." Arianna made a smug smile. "Someone should bring you back to your senses before you make a total fool of yourself."

"Just because I'm thinking positively, you want to tear me down." Megan turned to Mom. "And what about you? You're the one who made me watch *Shower of Power*. That's what got me thinking—"

"Instead of watching a show about a shower, you should be taking one." Arianna giggled. "Or maybe you're running for prom queen *pig*."

Megan grabbed her hairbrush and aimed it directly at Arianna's head.

"Go on out of here," Mom told Arianna. "And stop picking on your sister."

Arianna made loud grunting noises as she exited the room.

"Very mature!" Megan threw the hairbrush toward the door.

"Megan!" Mom scowled.

"I should've known you guys would be like this." Megan folded her arms across her chest, glaring at her mom.

"I'm sorry, Meggie. Really, I think it's, uh, very nice that you're setting such high goals for yourself." Her voice sounded stiff. "I just hope you won't be too terribly disappointed if you—"

"You're just as bad as Arianna!"

"I'm just trying to be realistic."

Megan covered her ears with her hands. "Pastor Robbie said not to listen to the naysayers in my life. He said there would be people who would try to discourage me. But I have to keep believing in myself, believing in my dreams. *Believe and receive*." She let out a deep sigh as she put her hands down. "And that's what I'm doing, Mom." She smiled hopefully. "Just wait and you'll see."

Mom made a weary nod as she left Megan's room. "I hope you're right, sweetheart."

"Maybe you should try it too," Megan called down the hallway to Mom.

Mom turned with a confused look. "I should run for prom queen?"

"No. You should work on your attitude toward life, Mom. A little more optimism wouldn't hurt you."

Mom tilted her head slightly, as if considering this advice. "You know, you just might be right about that. That's the thing I really do like about *Shower of Power* when I catch it on the radio. I know I need to be more upbeat, and I like

Pastor Robbie's positive outlook. I just need to implement it better."

Megan nodded. "Like with your job, Mom. No offense, but you're always complaining that no one appreciates you at work. Maybe you just need to appreciate yourself. It's time to start thinking more positively about yourself, and then others will too."

"Okay, I will do that." Mom got a twinkle in her eye. "In fact, I'm feeling very positive that you're going to go clean the kitchen this afternoon. Especially seeing how you're not sick anymore."

Megan rolled her eyes, then closed her door. It figured that her own family would treat her like this. Pastor Robbie said that it was those closest to you who would try to stomp on your dreams. As she taped her pages of schedule and lists on her wall, she was reminded of something from youth group a couple weeks ago. The youth pastor had talked about how some of Jesus's own family members had doubted him—and he was the Son of God. So, really, what did it matter if Mom and Arianna thought Megan was nuts for running for prom queen? Or even if her friends acted the same way? She would refuse to let their negativity bring her down. She would show them! Forty days from now, they would have to admit that they were wrong and she was right.

However, as she caught sight of her reflection in her mirrored closet doors, she was slightly taken aback. Perhaps Arianna was right about one thing: Megan could use a shower. Besides—she glanced at item number one in the "Improve Your Appearance" column—excellent daily hygiene was first on the list.

By Monday morning, Megan was ready to implement part one of her prom queen plan: "Friend Strategy." Fortunately, Megan already had a solid core of good, dependable friends from her youth group. Her plan was to announce her intentions to her closest friends at lunch today. Oh, she was prepared for their reaction. It probably would resemble what she'd received at home. To bolster her self-esteem and to help her friends see that she was sincere in this mission, she had taken great care in her appearance today. Her hair was clean and glossy. She was wearing a denim skirt from the Gap that Belinda had given her for Christmas, along with black tights and her favorite boots, topped with a burgundy sweater that everyone said looked great on her. She even put in earrings.

Megan had noticed that she and some of her friends had gotten used to dressing pretty sloppily this winter. It was probably because they were seniors and felt they had no one to impress, but Megan realized it was time to step up her game. Maybe she could even lead her friends to a higher fashion level while she was at it.

Her extra efforts didn't go unnoticed. Several of her friends mentioned that she looked nice. Janelle Parker even asked her if there was a guy involved in this new and improved appearance. This was ironic coming from Janelle since she'd never seemed to care much about her own look. In fact, Janelle often referred to herself as a "plain Jane."

"I'll answer you at lunch," Megan told her mysteriously.

As a result, her friends were all ears when she invited three of them to sit with her at what was not their usual table.

"Come on, out with it," Janelle insisted. "What's your big secret?"

"I have decided to run for prom queen." Megan waited for their reaction.

"Yeah, right." Janelle rolled her eyes. "Now tell us the truth. You're trolling for a boyfriend, aren't you? I heard that you've been flirting with Dayton Moore."

Megan firmly shook her head. "That's totally bogus. But I really am going to run for prom queen."

"Have you lost your ever-loving mind?" Lishia Vance demanded.

This actually hurt since Lishia was supposed to be Megan's best friend. Lishia used to be best friends with Janelle Parker. But that was before Chelsea Martin moved to town and shook things up. Oh, Chelsea was nice enough, but she was way too pretty—in that long-legged blonde sort of way that turned guys' heads. Megan just hoped Chelsea had no intention of running against her for prom queen, because Chelsea would probably have a very good chance of winning.

"I knew you guys would react like this," Megan calmly told them.

"Because it's insane." Lishia shoved a straw into her soda.

"Why are you doing this?" Janelle demanded. "Have you turned into a masochist? Or maybe you think you'll become a martyr."

"Or just a total fool." Lishia's brow creased, making her pixie-like features resemble a grumpy Smurf.

"Hey, you guys." Chelsea shook a finger at Janelle and Lishia. "Give Megan a chance to explain what she's thinking."

"Thinking?" Janelle laughed. "The girl has obviously lost it."

"There is obviously no thinking involved," Lishia added.

Megan restrained herself from reacting.

"Be quiet, you guys." Chelsea's voice grew firmer. "I want to hear what Megan has to say about this." She turned to Megan. "Go ahead now."

"Okay . . ." Megan took a deep breath, trying to remember what Pastor Robbie had said yesterday. "I'm trying to utilize the power of positive thinking. I think God has shown me that I've been too negative about myself."

"Well, that's true," Lishia admitted. "You usually are knocking yourself down."

Megan nodded. "That's right. And I'm going to put an end to it."

"But running for prom queen?" Janelle still looked skeptical. "What if you lose?"

"That's just it," Megan explained. "I can't think like that. I need to believe in myself, and I need to put everything I've got into this campaign."

"And if you lose?" Lishia pestered.

Megan held up her hand like a stop sign. "I don't want to hear that kind of negativity, okay? I'm sorry you don't get this, Lish. I just think it's something I really need to do. It would be nice to have your support, but if you want to—"

"I think it's great you are doing this," Chelsea interrupted. "I would absolutely vote for you, Megan."

"Really?" Megan blinked.

Chelsea nodded enthusiastically. "I'm always saying that just because we're Christians doesn't mean we should exclude ourselves from everything around us. Aren't we supposed to be an influence? How about what Jesus said about not hiding your light under a bushel basket? I think it's great you want to run for prom queen. I'd love to see a Christian in a position like that."

"Then why don't *you* run?" Janelle pointed at Chelsea. "You'd have a way better chance of making prom queen than—"

"That's not fair," Lishia shot back at Janelle. "Megan's the one who came up with this idea, so why are you trying to horn in on her—"

"It's a free election," Janelle argued back, and just like that, Lishia and Janelle, two girls who used to be best friends, were fighting over who should be running for prom queen and why or why not. Megan sat down and stuck a fork into her salad. This was another part of her plan—to eat more healthfully and hopefully take off a few pounds before the big event.

"Hang on, you two." Chelsea hit her fist on the table. "First of all, I do not *want* to run for prom queen, thank you very much, Janelle. I appreciate your support, but I'm not into that. Second of all, I want to help Megan run for prom queen. I think she'd be a great candidate."

"Really?" Megan couldn't believe her ears. Chelsea was the prettiest girl in their group of friends, maybe the prettiest girl in the whole school, and she wanted to help? "You'd actually do that?"

"Of course."

"I'll help you too," Lishia said in a slightly indignant tone.

Megan smiled at her. "I was hoping you would."

Janelle still looked unsure. "Have you seriously thought about this, Megan? I mean, do you have any idea what you're actually getting into?"

"You do remember that her sister was prom queen, don't you?" Lishia said defensively. "Of course Megan knows what she's getting into."

"Your sister was prom queen?" Chelsea looked surprised.

Janelle filled Chelsea in, then added, "But believe me, Belinda and Megan are as different as night and day. Some people would swear they're not even related." She laughed. "And some of us think that's a good thing."

"Thanks, I think." Megan made an uncomfortable smile.

"Is that why you want this?" Lishia asked cautiously. "Like you feel some weird, misplaced need to fill your sister's prom queen pumps?"

"Not at all. Belinda doesn't even know I'm doing this." Megan bit her lip, wondering what Belinda would say when she found out. "Although I'm sure I could get her to help me some—I mean, if she has time, since she is in college now."

"Well, I think you're very brave," Chelsea assured her. "And I meant what I said—I'd love to help you." She turned to the others. "You guys meant it too, right?"

"She'll need all the help she can get." Janelle took a bite of her burrito.

Suddenly Megan remembered her new mantra: *Act like you've already been crowned.* "Thank you so much." She graciously smiled at her friends. "You have no idea how much I appreciate all of you."

Lishia giggled. "Sheesh, Megan, you sound like you're giving your acceptance speech or something."

Megan forced a laugh. "I'll take that as a compliment." Thankfully, the conversation switched gears now. But as Megan sat there, eating her salad and listening to her friends, she felt more excited and hopeful than she'd felt in ages. She felt like her life was finally on track!

three

Megan's first official campaign planning meeting was scheduled for after school on Tuesday. However, Lishia had a yearbook meeting, so only Janelle and Chelsea were able to attend. To sweeten the deal, Megan offered to treat her friends to sundaes.

"Why are you having frozen yogurt?" Janelle gave Megan a suspicious look as they sat down with their sundaes.

"I'm trying to lose a few pounds before prom." Megan patted her midsection. "You and Chelsea are already skinny. But I need to watch the fats and calories."

"Are you working out?" Chelsea asked.

"Not exactly, but it's on my list." Megan opened her bag. "Speaking of lists, I brought some with me." She handed them each a copy. "These are the things I need to get done in the next few weeks."

Chelsea's eyes grew wide. "Wow, this is more involved than I realized."

"That's why it helps to get more people involved in the campaign," Megan explained. "I read that a prom queen campaign is no different than any other sort of political campaign. In fact, I got to thinking that if I enjoy this as much as I think I will, I might even go into politics."

Janelle's pink plastic spoon stopped just inches from her mouth. "You cannot be serious."

"Why not?" Megan shrugged. "I've always been interested in political science."

"You would actually run for public office, on purpose?"

"I think it's a great idea," Chelsea told Janelle. "We need more Christian leaders in politics. Don't you think?"

"I guess," Janelle said reluctantly.

"You know, Janelle," Megan said a bit cautiously, "it wouldn't hurt you to start thinking more positively."

Chelsea laughed and Janelle just rolled her eyes.

By the end of their meeting, Janelle had agreed to handle Megan's Facebook campaign, and Chelsea planned to help with posters.

"Since Lishia's not here, we'll assign her buttons," Megan said.

"We'll need to get some really good photos of you," Chelsea told her.

Megan frowned. "I'm not that photogenic."

"What happened to your positive thinking?" Janelle teased.

"Right." Megan nodded. "I am going to become very photogenic."

"We can help you with that," Chelsea offered.

"Oh, yeah," Megan said, "I heard how you made Janelle look so hot on that youth group retreat last fall." She pointed at Janelle. "So why don't you look like that all the time?"

Janelle made a face. "Because I happen to be perfectly fine with my appearance, thank you very much. I know that beauty is only skin deep. And I'd rather improve my mind than obsess over my outward looks."

Megan controlled herself from sniping back. Reminding herself of one of her slogans—*a prom queen is gracious and kind to everyone*—she simply smiled and nodded. "That's very admirable."

Janelle laughed. "There she goes again, putting on her prom queen act."

"Being polite doesn't have to be an act," Megan replied. "Maybe I just want to become a nicer person. Is there anything wrong with that?"

"Not if it's genuine," Janelle told her.

"Anyway, back to the photos," Megan said to Chelsea. "Do you think you can help me with that? Maybe a little makeover?"

Chelsea nodded. "Sure, it'd be fun. But we don't want to go too far with it. The whole point that Janelle and I were trying to make at the retreat is that everyone is too focused on looks. And there's no way I want to turn you into a jerk magnet."

"Huh?" Megan frowned. "A jerk magnet?"

Janelle giggled. "No chance of that, Chelsea. Short of the kind of costume I was wearing, Megan doesn't have what it takes to become a jerk magnet."

"What is a jerk magnet?" Megan asked.

Chelsea and Janelle took turns explaining how some girls

have a certain look—a look that magically attracts guys who are only interested in one thing.

"You know the kind of girl, really pretty with all the right kinds of curves and a mane of long, blonde hair," Janelle told her. "A guy takes one look at her and assumes she's auditioning to be his personal playmate."

Megan nodded. "Well, that's definitely not the look I'm going for, so don't worry." She pointed to Chelsea. "To be honest, the first time I met you last fall . . . well, I kind of thought you were one of those girls. But I know now I was wrong. Besides, you've kind of toned it down."

"Thanks." Chelsea dropped her spoon into her empty sundae cup. "I had to learn that the hard way. Kate—that's my stepmom—she kind of helped me with a makeover that went a little too far. Trust me, I'm glad not to look like that anymore. Besides it being too time consuming, it's a relief to not feel like a jerk magnet."

"Nicholas Prague seems to appreciate it." Megan knew that Chelsea and Nicholas were "almost" going together.

Chelsea grinned. "For sure. Did you know that he was totally put off by the way I looked before?"

Megan shook her head. "That's hard to believe."

"Speaking of guys, have you considered your date for prom?" Janelle asked.

Megan shrugged. "Not exactly."

"Well, I hope it's on your list," Janelle teased. "It'd probably be embarrassing to be a dateless prom queen."

"How about you?" Megan decided to defer this. "Who will you go to prom with—I mean, if you go?"

Now Janelle looked uneasy.

"Chase will probably ask her," Chelsea said. "Hey, maybe we could double-date with you guys."

"Good idea," Janelle said with enthusiasm. "Tell Nicholas to start putting a bug in Chase's ear, and we can all go together."

Suddenly Janelle and Chelsea were discussing their plans for prom, and Megan felt like an outsider. Still, she knew she couldn't get mad about it. At least not in front of them. So she just sat and listened, trying not to imagine herself as the dateless prom queen. Really, she would need to start working on that important ingredient too.

Before they parted ways, Chelsea promised to figure out the makeover and photo shoot. "Maybe this weekend," she suggested. "I'll see if Kate is available. She's a good photographer and pretty smart about makeovers too."

"Just don't turn me into a jerk magnet," Megan said in a joking tone as she unlocked her car.

"No worries there." Chelsea waved.

Megan got into her car and let out a big sigh. This running for prom queen thing was starting to feel like a part-time job. But, she reminded herself, the payoff would be worth it. Suddenly she noticed something in her car. Oh, it had been there since she'd been allowed to start driving this car last fall, after Belinda went to college, but it felt like the first time she'd actually seen it. Hanging on the rearview mirror, dangling on a faded pink ribbon, was a gold heart. Actually it was a plastic heart, but it was supposed to look like gold. Embossed in the center of the heart in teeny tiny letters were the words "I Believe."

Megan remembered how she'd made fun of Belinda last

year. Her sister's prom queen slogan, "Believe in Belinda," had not only sounded lame to Megan but sacrilegious too. Not that Megan's opinions had influenced Belinda in the least. But now here Megan was, not only driving what used to be Belinda's car but attempting to imitate her sister in her quest for prom queen too.

As Megan put the car into gear, she wondered if there might be something wrong with this unexpected development. Was she making a big mistake in getting into this whole prom queen business? Was she becoming shallow and superficial, the very things she used to tease Belinda for? Or was this just those "pesky naysayer doubts" that Pastor Robbie had preached about? As she drove over to the middle school to pick up Arianna from soccer practice, she decided not to listen to the negativity. After all, she already had three friends who were willing to help and support her in this campaign. She couldn't let them down. She couldn't turn back now. She was not going to let those negative needles pop her balloon.

"Why are you late?" Arianna demanded as she threw her pack into the backseat of the car.

"I'm not late," Megan shot back. Of course, this instigated an argument, but glancing at the clock on the dash, Megan decided to concede. "Okay, so I was ten minutes late, Arianna. Sorry." Fortunately, that shut her baby sister up.

"Are you still planning to run for prom queen?" Arianna asked.

Megan was trying to decipher her tone. Was Arianna getting ready to launch into tease mode again? Did it even matter? "Yes," she said slowly. "I'm still planning to run for prom queen. In fact, that's why I'm late. I was having a planning meeting."

"A planning meeting?"

Figuring this was good practice at congeniality, Megan explained the nature of the meeting and what her friends were offering to do, including the makeover and photo shoot.

"That's cool." Arianna nodded. "Sounds like fun."

Megan concealed her surprise. "Yeah, I think so too."

"But I'm still a little confused."

"Confused?" Megan braced herself for a snitty sister attack.

"Last year when Belinda was running for prom queen, you constantly made fun of her. You even told her she was acting like an oversized Barbie doll. You called her *Belinda Barbie*, remember?"

Megan grimaced. "Yeah, now that you mention it, I do remember."

"Why did you think that then? And what makes it any different now?"

Megan thought about it. "Those are good questions."

"Uh-huh." Arianna was peeling open a granola bar wrapper. "Got any good answers?"

"To be honest, I suppose I was jealous of Belinda."

"Uh-huh." She nodded and took a bite.

"I suppose I owe her an apology."

"Maybe so," Arianna said with a full mouth.

"And the reason I want to run now . . . ?"

"Yeah. Why?"

"The truth is, I really want to start thinking more positively about myself. I want to believe in myself and that I'm able to accomplish something big."

"So you're really serious about prom queen?"

Megan nodded. "I am."

"Cool. Well, let me know if I can help. Olivia would probably help again too. Remember we made buttons for Belinda last year."

"That's right. You guys are like the button pros."

"Of course, Belinda did pay us in pizza and videos and stuff."

"Sounds like a deal to me." Still pretending she was already prom queen, Megan decided to ask Arianna about her day. "How was soccer practice?"

As Arianna opened up, going on and on about how stupid Felicity Gossler was acting like the world's worst prima donna and like their team wouldn't survive one game without her, Megan realized that putting on this whole prom queen persona had some unexpected perks. Not only was Megan learning how to exercise tact and diplomacy, but everyone around her seemed to be acting a little nicer too. There really was power in positive thinking!

four

Over the next few days, Megan went out of her way to be friendly with everyone who crossed her path. Sometimes she received pleasantly surprising results, like when Dayton Moore complimented her on her outfit (somewhat concerning since she was wearing a T-shirt that Mom had accidentally shrunk in the dryer), but then he asked her to help him with an essay. Dayton was an athletic hero but something of an academic zero. Not that it had seemed to trouble him much. But unfortunately his senior year had become a challenge because he needed to have at least passing grades to get into the small college that was offering him a football scholarship.

"I'll help you with your essay," she promised him, "if you'll help me to campaign for prom queen."

He looked somewhat shocked. "You're running for prom queen?"

She placed a forefinger over her lips and grinned. "Don't tell."

"Uh, okay. But I heard that Amanda Jorgenson was going to be prom queen this year."

Megan frowned. "How could anyone possibly know that? It's an election, Dayton. The students get to vote for prom queen."

He gave her a blank look.

"You think it's no contest?"

Now he shrugged.

"Do you want help with your essay or not?"

He grinned. "Yeah, sure."

"So you'll help me in my campaign?" She smiled sweetly.

"Sure." He nodded. "Why not? Amanda wins everything. It's about time someone else had a shot."

Megan knew that Dayton had dated Amanda some time ago and that Amanda had been the one to dump him. He'd likely never gotten over it. Perhaps Megan could work that in her favor.

Megan and Dayton shook hands on this new alliance, and Megan headed off to choir feeling like she was at the top of her game. But on her way, she noticed Zoë Evanston standing in the shadows of the music building. Zoë and Megan had been friends back in grade school, but by middle school Zoë had started getting wild, and they parted ways. She hadn't had a real conversation with Zoë in years.

"Hey, Zoë," she said in a friendly tone.

Zoë just glared at her.

"I haven't seen you around much," Megan persisted, trying not to stare at the huge silver lip ring and numerous eyebrow studs. Didn't Zoë know how ridiculous that stuff made her look? The black leather jacket didn't help much either. "How's it going?"

"What do you care?" Zoë shot at her.

Megan's smile faded. "I was just saying hi."

"Well, save it for someone who gives a—"

"Sorry." Megan held up her hands. "Excuse me for being friendly."

Now Zoë stepped out in front of Megan, putting her hands on her hips and blocking the path. "Friendly?" Zoë demanded. "You think you're friendly? Give me a break, you stuck-up—"

"Why are you so angry?" Megan nervously glanced around to see if anyone was nearby to witness this unexpected little scene. Not that she was particularly worried, but the dark, threatening look on Zoë's face was a little scary. And hearing the tardy bell ring suggested that everyone else, or at least the law-abiding students, had probably gone to class.

"Maybe I'm sick of people like you," Zoë practically spat into Megan's face. "Maybe I wish people like you would just bug off and leave people like me alone."

"Okay." Megan stepped back. "Excuse me."

"I would if I could think of one." With dark, narrowed eyes, Zoë stepped aside and let loose with some off-color language. As Megan scurried past, jogging to the choir room, she figured she probably wouldn't be getting Zoë's vote this year.

❧

By the end of the week, Megan knew she had her work cut out for her. She hadn't gone public in her quest for prom queen yet; only her closest friends were in the loop. But her "make new friends" campaign definitely had its challenges. She found that she received several different reactions. Although most of her peers returned her friendliness in kind, a number of them responded with indifference, some acted suspicious, and a few others, like Zoë, were downright hostile.

"This isn't as easy as I thought it would be," she confessed to Chelsea on Friday night. The four friends had gathered for a makeover-sleepover. Chelsea's stepmom Kate had taught them some beginning yoga steps, and a friend of Kate's had demonstrated some products and shown them how to give each other facials. Now, with their paste-covered faces in various stages of treatment, they were just finishing up an old Sandra Bullock movie, *Miss Congeniality*.

"Whether or not you run for prom queen, I think this has been fun," Lishia told Megan.

"It would be more fun if we had some good old-fashioned junk food." Janelle held her carrot stick like a cigar. "Instead of this rabbit chow."

"Kate thought it would be helpful to detox," Chelsea whispered. "You know, so that our complexions would look good. But I hid some goodies in my room for later. I figured we'd be dying of hunger."

"Hunger," Lishia said suddenly. "That reminds me, I signed up to work at the soup kitchen tomorrow for lunch. Anyone else going? I could use a ride downtown."

"My mom committed me to babysit for my aunt tomorrow afternoon," Janelle told her. "Believe me, I'd rather be at the soup kitchen than with my bratty cousins."

"I'll go with you to the soup kitchen," Chelsea offered. "I've been meaning to sign up for it, and it'll be more fun going with someone I know."

"Maybe I should go too," Megan said. "In fact, I actually need to find some kind of a good cause."

"A good cause?" Lishia made a confused frown.

"You know, for prom queen," Megan told her. "A good prom queen candidate always has a good cause. It's part of being well-rounded."

"Speaking of well-rounded, I need junk food!" Janelle proclaimed. The girls raced up to Chelsea's room, where they put in another movie and totally pigged out. Megan, however, practiced some restraint. She knew that if she wanted to be a serious contender for prom queen, she had to get into better shape. And a little past midnight, she decided that if she wanted to be photogenic in the morning, she'd better get some beauty sleep. So despite her friends' attempt to pull an all-nighter, Megan called it a night and slipped over to the guest room across the hall where she went to sleep.

The next morning, Chelsea and Kate went to work giving Megan her makeover. Between hair, makeup, and a black sequined dress that once belonged to Belinda, Megan actually felt surprisingly pretty by the time Kate began to take photos of her. Of course, the shots wouldn't reveal how the dress was gaping in back. Unable to get the zipper up on the fitted garment, Chelsea had come to the rescue with safety pins.

With all her friends urging her to strike poses and ham it up while the camera clicked, Megan realized she was actually having a good time. Halfway through the session, she switched out of the black number for a red silky dress she'd worn to homecoming last year. This dress actually fit and was easier to move around in.

"This is so out of my comfort zone," Megan confessed to Kate after they finally finished up. "It's always been my older sister who does this kind of thing. She's the pretty one. Belinda loves posing for the camera."

"Sounds like it's your turn for the limelight." Kate put her camera lens away.

"Thanks," Megan told her. "Thanks so much for everything!"

"It's time to head over to the soup kitchen," Lishia announced. She pointed to Megan. "Do you want to change first?"

Megan shrugged. The truth was, she wasn't ready to give up the red dress quite yet. It was fun feeling this pretty. And after all, wasn't she supposed to act like she was already the prom queen? "I think I'll just go as I am," she said on impulse. "Maybe the people at the soup kitchen will enjoy seeing something like this. Add a little color to their world."

Chelsea looked uncertain and Janelle rolled her eyes. "Whatever," Lishia said as she started stuffing some clothes into her bag. "But we need to get moving."

As they gathered up their things, Megan was having second thoughts. Perhaps going to the soup kitchen in a red silk dress was a bit much. "Maybe I should change," she said as they were heading outside.

"There's no time now," Lishia insisted. "We have to be there at eleven."

As Megan drove them downtown, she felt a little silly for not having changed clothes. Both Chelsea and Lishia were wearing jeans. Really, what had she been thinking? So after parking in back, she grabbed her bag, thinking she'd take a few moments to change her clothes once they were inside.

"Here comes our girl now," a gray-haired woman called out as Lishia led them into the kitchen. "It looks like she's brought helpers too."

"Good thing since we're shorthanded today," a skinny bald guy said.

Suddenly the gray-haired woman, Bertie, was shouting out orders. Lishia was sent out to set up tables and chairs, Chelsea was put in charge of a big mixer, and Megan was instructed to peel potatoes.

"You seem a mite overdressed for the kitchen," Bertie said as she handed Megan an apron.

"Yeah, we don't usually get kitchen help this fancy." The bald guy chuckled. "We'll have to let you be a server today. Might impress our guests."

"I, uh, I was going to change." Megan nodded to the bag she'd tossed in a corner. "I have some jeans—"

"Not now," Bertie told her. "Right now we need to get those taters peeled and into the oven."

Megan focused on the potatoes, peeling as fast as she could and the whole time feeling out of place, conspicuous, and slightly silly. Finally, when the last potato was peeled, she started to take off the apron.

"Not yet," Bertie told her. "Those taters need to be cut first." She grabbed a knife and cutting board and demonstrated how she wanted the potatoes sliced. "Unless this is too hard for the fancy girl to do." Bertie chuckled, but her brow creased with what looked like disapproval.

"No, no, it's okay," Megan assured her. She started slicing the potatoes and layering them in the oversized aluminum pan Bertie had set nearby. She could hear the others busily working too, chatting and joking cheerfully. But as she sliced and layered, she felt strangely removed from them, as if she had separated herself from everyone else simply by deciding to wear this silly red dress.

Finally the last potato slice was in the pan, and Megan laid down the knife. "I'll just go and change now," she said quietly. Thankfully no one tried to stop her as she grabbed her bag and went off in search of the ladies' room. But when she found the restroom, she also found a line of women waiting to use it. She could tell by their clothes and conversation that they were either homeless or down on their luck.

"Looks like someone must've had a busy night," a young woman said when Megan went to the end of the line. The woman with her laughed loudly, and an older woman told them both to shut up.

"I used to be real pretty too." The older woman patted her thinning brown hair, revealing a set of dirty fingernails. "A girl's got to do what a girl's got to do."

The younger women snickered, and Megan stood a little straighter. Were they suggesting what she thought they were suggesting?

"Don't pay no attention to them," the older woman told Megan. "They're probably just jealous."

"Excuse me." Megan backed away from the line. "I, uh, I don't really need to use the restroom after all." She hurried outside and shoved her bag into the trunk of her car. Why had she agreed to do this? Would anyone care if she just left?

She could call Lishia's cell and make up an excuse. But that would leave them without a ride. No, Megan decided, better to stick it out. Isn't that what a prom queen would do? Holding her head high, she returned to the kitchen where she was now given the task of peeling carrots.

"This is really fun," Chelsea called out. "I think I'll become a regular here."

Megan glanced over her shoulder to see Chelsea scooping batter from the big mixing bowl and pouring it into muffin cups. It didn't really look like much fun, although it had to be better than being stuck at the sink. Megan felt like the peeler queen. Finally, after what seemed like hours, it was time to serve up the food, and Bertie, true to her word, insisted that Megan should be a server. Megan tried to talk her out of it, but Bertie wouldn't back down.

"You look so festive." She gave her a firm but gentle shove. "You go on out there and cheer up the good folks. You can dish up them taters you helped make."

Wearing a forced smile and vinyl gloves, Megan took her place in the serving area and obediently scooped out the scalloped potatoes. But instead of the diners being cheered up, it seemed that they just looked at her with suspicion and maybe even hostility. If she didn't put enough potatoes on their plates, they let her know. However, when they got down to where Chelsea was handing out muffins and cheerful chatter, they actually thanked her. How Chelsea was able to act like she was having a good time was a mystery to Megan. The sooner she finished up here, the happier she would be.

It was close to three o'clock by the time the kitchen was cleaned up and the girls were excused from their stint of volunteering. As they walked out to the car, Megan's feet were killing her, and her favorite pair of heels were now splattered with pieces of vegetable peelings. Why hadn't she at least thought to change her shoes? Megan felt completely drained as she started the car. "Are you guys as exhausted as I am?" she asked.

"Exhausted?" Chelsea shook her head. "Not really. In fact, I actually feel kind of invigorated. I mean, it was work, but I had fun."

"Me too," Lishia agreed. "That was very cool."

Megan said nothing. Keeping her eyes on the road, she focused on her driving as she took her friends to their homes, but as she dropped them off, she pasted on her prom queen smile and tried to pretend she'd had as good a time as they claimed to have had. When she got home, she peeled off what looked like a completely ruined dress, collapsed into her bed, and fell asleep.

five

"That was so nice of you to help at the soup kitchen," Mom said as they went to church the next morning.

Megan just nodded as she checked messages on her phone.

"I've considered doing it myself, but I'm usually so wiped out by the weekend that the idea of working isn't too appealing," Mom admitted. "So how was it?"

"Hard work," Megan mumbled.

"How old do you have to be to do it?" Arianna asked from the backseat.

"I think you're old enough," Mom said as she pulled into the church lot. "Maybe you can go with Megan next time she—"

"There's not going to be a next time." Megan turned off her phone and slipped it into her bag.

"Why not?" Arianna asked as they got out of the car.

Megan shrugged. "It's just not my kind of thing."

"Too bad." Mom closed the door. "It's a nice way to help out the community."

"Well, I came up with another idea for helping the homeless," Megan said as they walked toward the church.

"Really?" Mom peered curiously at her.

"Yeah. I just decided last night that I'm going to do a fundraiser." Megan's plan was to make it part of her prom queen campaign. She hoped to raise enough money to get an article in the paper or maybe even a spot on the news.

"What kind of fundraiser?" Arianna asked. "What're you going to do?"

"I haven't decided yet," Megan admitted.

Now they went their separate ways—Mom to the service, Arianna to the middle school group, and Megan joining her high school friends in the basement where the music was blasting loudly.

"How come you didn't make it to youth group last night?" Lishia asked her. "I called and texted you."

"I know. Sorry. I fell asleep and then it was too late," Megan said as they went to find seats. The first part of youth group was always music and singing, and Megan usually enjoyed it, but today she was distracted. Although she mouthed the words, her brain was busily preparing a little speech she planned to give during the prayer and praise session.

"Okay, guys, that was great," Raymond, the youth leader, said as he took the stage. "Let's give a hand to our worship team. Great job!" Everyone clapped, and then the room slowly grew quiet.

"All right, it's time for prayer and praise, and I have a good praise report to start us out." Raymond shared about a friend of his who they'd all been praying for and how his cancer had just gone into remission. Everyone clapped. Now Megan shot her hand up.

"Megan Bernard," Raymond called out.

She stood with a nervous smile. "I want to ask everyone here to pray for me. I've decided to do something way outside of my comfort zone. Now, don't laugh, you guys." She paused, taking in a breath. "I have decided to run for prom queen at Kingston High." There were a few snickers, and Raymond made a stern face. "The reason I'm asking for prayer is because I want to do this for God. I want God to be glorified in me while I campaign. Also, I'm going to do a fundraiser for the homeless people in our community. I'd really appreciate everyone's prayers and support for that too." She smiled. "Thank you!"

Megan sat down and realized her legs were actually trembling. Lishia patted her on the shoulder, and Megan let out a relieved sigh. Glad that was over, she tried to focus on the other prayer requests and praise reports, but she was distracted with her own thoughts now. Trying to decide what she should do for her fundraiser, she began running various ideas through her head. She'd found some good websites with suggestions for fundraising.

Her big question was which idea would cost the least and raise the most money. She needed to figure it out ASAP if she wanted it to wrap up just one week before the election in order to impress everyone. According to what she'd read, two weeks was about the perfect amount of time for a fundraiser when items were being sold. Not too long, not too short. However, she also needed to promote the fundraiser for at least a week or two before it actually started. That meant she needed to decide what she planned to do by Monday!

Basically there were several different categories of fundraisers. She could buy products and sell them, but that meant money up front, and what if she couldn't sell them all? Or she could plan some kind of big one-night event. That could be anything from a spaghetti feed to a Mardi Gras party. Or there were the sponsoring kinds of events like bowl-athons or dance-athons. The question was—which one to do?

"That was a good message, huh?" Lishia said as the meeting came to an end.

Megan nodded and tried to remember, but she honestly couldn't recall a single word that had been spoken. To cover this, she began to ask Lishia what she thought about her fundraiser ideas. "Right now I'm leaning toward a one-night event," she explained. "Although some kind of a marathon event might be cheaper and easier. You know, like a walk-athon."

A pretty girl named Bethany Bridgewater shyly approached them. Megan didn't know Bethany that well but thought she was a sweet girl. Besides that, Bethany was one more potential vote for her. "Hey, Bethany." Megan greeted her like a long-lost friend. "It's good to see you. What's up?"

"I like what you're doing to help the homeless people, and I just wanted to volunteer to help out. I mean, if you need any help."

"That's great," Megan told her.

"We never refuse extra help," Lishia added.

Bethany explained how she belonged to a show choir group called Joyful Sound. "It's a song and dance group that sometimes performs at nursing homes and places like that. We like to encourage people through music," she told Megan. "Maybe we could do something for your fundraiser event." Bethany waved to a blonde girl who was approaching. "This is my best friend Summer, and she's in this group too." Bethany told Summer her idea, and Summer agreed it would be a fun event.

"That's great," Megan told both of them. "I'm sure having you guys perform would make the fundraiser even more special."

As Bethany and Summer went to talk to some of their friends, Chelsea and Nicholas, followed by Chase and Janelle, came over to join Megan and Lishia. The whole group started talking about Raymond's message and their interpretations of it. Normally this was the kind of conversation Megan would enjoy and participate in, but all she could do was nod as she feigned interest, because her mind was on the fundraiser and how she wanted it to be a big success. Finally there was a lull, and she decided to jump in. "What do you guys think about bingo?" she blurted out.

"*Bingo?*" Nicholas frowned. "What are you talking about?"

She giggled. "For a fundraiser. I was thinking about a bingo night. Maybe combined with a chili feed. Do you think that's too hokey?"

"Bingo and chili?" Chase cocked his head to one side. "Sounds like something my great-aunt Lou-Lou might enjoy."

Everyone laughed.

"How about a dance-athon?" Megan tried.

"What's the money going to?" Nicholas asked.

"To the homeless," she explained. "Weren't you listening to me during the prayer and praise?"

"I was putting away my guitar," he explained.

"Oh, yeah." She'd forgotten that he was on the worship team this morning.

"How are you going to get the money to the homeless?" Nicholas persisted.

"Yeah, you can't just hit the streets and start handing out twenties," Chase teased. "Although I'm sure the homeless wouldn't mind."

"How about donating it to the soup kitchen?" Chelsea suggested. Then she started telling the guys and Janelle about how cool it had been to help out, and the next thing Megan knew, they were all traipsing over to the church foyer to find the sign-up sheet for soup kitchen volunteers.

"Aren't you going to sign up?" Lishia asked Megan as she hung back.

"I think I'll have enough on my plate with the fundraiser," Megan said. "But maybe I will donate the funds to the soup kitchen. Do you think they'd like that?"

"I don't see why they wouldn't. I heard Bertie saying they were running out of some supplies, kind of like she was hoping that someone would bring something by. She said the soup kitchen was a faith-based ministry."

"Does that mean you've decided to dedicate your fundraiser to the soup kitchen?" Chelsea asked as she joined them.

Megan nodded. "Yeah. I think that's the plan." She invited all of them to meet with her after school tomorrow to start planning for the fundraiser. "There's really no time to waste," she informed them. "Lishia said they're running out of food." Unfortunately, the guys were just starting spring soccer and had practice, but the girls promised to come.

"I have to say, a fundraiser for the soup kitchen is something I can really get behind," Janelle told Megan. "That's a really great idea."

Lishia told the others about Bethany Bridgewater's offer to help and her suggestion to have their song and dance group perform. "It could be really fun."

Megan just hoped she could come up with a doable fundraising idea that everyone could get excited about. To that end, she spent the afternoon surfing the internet and reading everything she could find about fundraising. But the more she read, the more discouraged she felt. It wasn't until Sunday evening that she realized she still had homework. Finally, before going to bed, she texted her friends and asked each one of them to come to the meeting with a specific fundraiser idea, explaining that they would vote on the best one. "Diplomacy," she said as she turned off her phone and plugged it into the charger.

On Monday afternoon, Megan was pleased to see that her friends actually did have some fundraising ideas. This time they met at the coffeehouse, Megan's treat. First of all, Janelle suggested a golf tournament. "My dad even offered to invite a bunch of his friends," she told them. "He's good friends with the owner of Breckenridge and thinks it would be a great place for it."

"Interesting." Megan wrote this down but immediately crossed it off in her mind. A golf tournament? Really, what high school kid wants to be involved in that? The golf team?

"I think we should do a casino night," Lishia suggested. "My mom knows where you can rent all the gambling equipment, and they set it all up in the gym or cafeteria, and everyone dresses up. It would be fun, and it sounds like you can make a boatload of money."

"Gambling?" Megan frowned. "I don't know if that's such a good idea. Some people think gambling is wrong."

"Gambling for a good cause," Lishia pointed out. "People plunk down their money, play games, and then you have prizes for them to win."

"What's your idea?" Megan turned to Chelsea.

"Stone soup," Chelsea said.

"Huh?" Megan frowned. "What's stone soup?"

"You know," Chelsea told her, "everyone brings one food item, and you put it all together to make a big pot of soup. Then you sell the soup for, say, ten bucks a bowl."

"You think people would show up with a carrot or potato and pay ten dollars for a bowl of soup?" Megan was incredulous.

"It would be stone soup and a silent auction," Chelsea explained. "People pay for their soup, drop off their items, and then while the soup is cooking, they walk around and make bids on the silent auction items."

"And where do we get those items?" Megan asked.

"The few weeks before the auction, we invite people in the community to donate things."

"That sounds pretty cool," Lishia told her. "I'd go to an event like that."

"Okay, now tell us your idea," Janelle urged Megan.

"How about spaghetti karaoke?"

"Spaghetti karaoke?" Janelle frowned.

"People buy tickets to the spaghetti dinner, and then we have a karaoke contest with prizes that will entice people to buy a karaoke ticket. Not only do we make more money that way, but the karaoke will provide us with entertainment too." Megan smiled happily. "Doesn't that sound like fun?"

"Not so much." Janelle wrinkled her nose. "It actually sounds kind of torturous, eating spaghetti and being forced to listen to bad karaoke. Do you sell them Tums as they're leaving?"

Lishia and Chelsea laughed.

"I really like the stone soup idea," Lishia said. "It's kind of laid-back. And a stone soup fundraiser to benefit the soup kitchen—it kind of makes sense, you know?"

"How about my golf tournament idea?" Janelle asked. "It could bring in some big bucks."

"But the only people involved would be golfers," Megan pointed out. "Shouldn't a fundraiser be something that everyone wants to participate in?"

"Like karaoke," Janelle said sarcastically.

"You guys really don't like the karaoke idea?" Megan peered at her friends' faces, but it was obvious they hated it. So she put the four suggestions to a vote, and Chelsea's idea won. Stone soup and a silent auction it would be. But the truth was, Megan thought it was rather unimpressive.

However, it did give her an idea for delegating. "Since your fundraiser won," she said to Chelsea, "and since you probably have some specific thoughts on how to carry it out, why don't you take the lead?"

"Sure," Chelsea agreed. "Like Lishia said, the stone soup part is pretty simple. I think that's the beauty of it. But we might also want to get some cakes and pies donated so we could sell desserts and coffee too. Of course, we'll need a place to host the event. Probably a place with a kitchen, although we might be able to cook the soup at another location and bring in disposable bowls and utensils."

"I have an idea," Lishia said suddenly. "I heard about another school doing this once. Art students made all these different bowls, and they served soup in the handmade bowls and sold the soup and the bowls together, probably for more than ten bucks too."

"That's a fantastic idea!" Chelsea said.

"I can ask Mrs. Steiner about it in art tomorrow," Lishia offered. "If we got right on it, we could probably have quite a few bowls done in a few weeks."

"We need to have the fundraiser by the first week in May," Megan pointed out.

"Why?"

"Because it needs to be all wrapped up the week before the prom election."

Janelle slapped her forehead. "I almost forgot that there was an ulterior motive here. I actually thought we were doing this for the soup kitchen."

"We are," Megan said defensively.

"Yeah, right." Janelle's tone was still sarcastic.

"What difference does it make that the prom got us thinking about a fundraiser for the soup kitchen?" Chelsea asked. "The important thing is that we're doing it. In fact, we should be grateful that Megan is running for prom queen because that's why this is going to happen, right?"

"Right." Lishia nodded.

"I guess." Janelle made a resolute sigh.

"Back to the plans. I'll see if we can have the event in the school cafeteria," Megan said. "If that doesn't work, I'm sure the church will let us do it there, although that won't hold as many people." She made some notes. "But my biggest question is, where do we get stuff for the silent auction?" She looked at Chelsea.

"We invite people in the community to donate things," Chelsea explained. "Like an artist might donate a painting. A restaurant could donate a meal. I'll even ask my dad to donate some designer clothes or a gift certificate from his shops."

"I can get into that," Lishia said with enthusiasm.

"We'll obviously want things with some value," she continued. "And nothing used, unless it's an antique or collectible."

"It sounds like you've given this some serious thought," Janelle told her.

"Before my mom died, she put on a silent auction fundraiser for a youth ministry in our area."

"Do you have a specific plan for getting things donated?" Megan asked. "I mean, because you're new in town, do you know enough people to approach? It seems like it might take a lot of begging and coercing to gather enough stuff for a real auction."

"I'll help her," Janelle offered.

Megan jotted this in her notes. "Okay, then. Chelsea and Janelle will handle the silent auction and stone soup. Lishia will check on the handmade bowls. I'll find a location and decide on a date. Now we need to make a plan for getting the word out."

"I can design the posters," Chelsea said.

"I can ask my aunt about putting some ads on the radio," Janelle offered. "She manages a Christian radio station. Maybe they'll want to donate the time since it's for such a good cause."

"And I'll check out getting something on television and in the newspaper," Megan said.

They went over a few more details, and then Megan switched gears by bringing up her prom queen campaign. "My little sister and her friend volunteered to make buttons for me," she told them. "But I don't have a slogan yet."

"That reminds me, I just put together some layouts for your prom queen posters last night," Chelsea said. "And I already loaded some of the photos from Saturday. I think they look awesome, but you'll need to check them out."

"I can't wait to see."

"I'll bring my laptop to school tomorrow," Chelsea promised. "Maybe we can use some of the elements on your buttons too."

"Very cool." Megan paused to sip her mocha and check her list. "How's the social media coming, Janelle?"

"I set up a Facebook page for you. It's called 'Kings Queen Megan.'"

"Kings Queen Megan?"

"Kings for Kingston, you know. It was the best I could do." Janelle pointed to Chelsea. "Maybe you can load some of those photos onto it. I'll send you the password."

Megan beamed at them. "You guys are all awesome. I really appreciate your help. And just so you know, I'm recruiting some others to help too. In fact, Dayton Moore even offered his assistance."

"Dayton?" Chelsea looked surprised.

"What on earth is Dayton going to do?" Janelle demanded.

"I read that a successful prom queen recruits a wide variety of volunteers. You broaden your base by having kids from all walks involved."

"And Dayton *offered* to help?" Chelsea still looked doubtful.

"Actually he offered in return for me helping him with an essay. Favor for a favor."

"That reminds me." Janelle narrowed her eyes. "I just overheard Dayton's ex-girlfriend telling someone that she plans to make a run for the crown too."

"Riley Atkins?" Megan asked.

"Not that ex," Janelle told her.

"Oh, you mean Amanda."

"No, not that ex either." Janelle laughed. "I wonder if there will ever be an ex club for all the girls Dayton has gone out with during high school. Anyway, I'm talking about his latest ex, Hallie Bennett."

"Oh, yeah, I almost forgot her. They didn't go out for long. Hallie is running for prom queen?" Megan frowned. Hallie was not one of Megan's favorite people. Not even close. The girl had been acting superior for years. Seriously, she was usually a total snob to anyone not in her tight circle of friends. But she was also very, very pretty.

Janelle nodded grimly.

"It figures." Lishia shook her head.

Janelle turned to Megan. "To be honest, I was never that into this whole prom queen campaign. But when I heard Hallie saying that, well, I decided that I'd be really glad to see you beat her."

"Me too," Lishia said with enthusiasm. "No way can we

let Hallie win this thing. I'll do everything I can to help you, Megan."

"What's the deal with Hallie?" Chelsea asked Lishia. "You guys sound like you really hate her."

"Hate is a strong word," Megan said carefully.

Lishia sighed. "I know, and I've really tried to forgive her. But sometimes I just . . . well, anyway, I just hope she's not prom queen."

"What did Hallie *do*?" Chelsea asked curiously.

"You mean besides being stuck-up and mean?" Janelle pointed to Lishia now. "Let's just say that Hallie and Lishia go way back."

"Huh?" Chelsea was clearly confused. "Way back to when?"

"To grade school," Janelle said.

"Yeah," Megan added. "It was a really bad slumber party in fourth grade."

"Please, don't remind me." Lishia rolled her eyes. "Or I might forget I'm a Christian and start hating her all over again."

"Now I'm really curious." Chelsea looked hopefully at them. "I've told you guys some of my bad grade-school stories."

"Trust me, none of your stories are as bad as this one," Lishia assured her.

"Come on," Chelsea urged.

"It has to do with a bowl of water," Janelle said quietly to Chelsea. "Lishia was the first girl to go to sleep."

"I had a kidney problem as a kid," Lishia said with irritation.

"Hallie took a photo with her phone and posted it on MySpace for everyone to see," Megan added.

"Get the picture?" Janelle asked.

Chelsea gave Lishia a sympathetic sideways hug. "Very mean."

"Anyway, this might actually be good news about Hallie running," Megan said suddenly.

"How's that?" Chelsea asked.

"It might help to split the vote between Amanda and her. Those girls are in the same clique." Megan drew a circle and divided it in half, then divided one half into quarters, writing Hallie and Amanda in the quarter pieces and her name in the half. "See, I might get the rest of the votes."

Janelle laughed. "That seems overly simplistic to me."

"It might work." Megan closed her notebook and pulled out a couple of pages she'd printed from an online site. One showed chocolate bars that could be packaged with her name and photo on them. The other page was for pencils and pens with her name on them. "I was thinking about ordering something to give to voters," she explained. "Candy bars seem like a no-brainer since most people like chocolate. Except that the wrappers with my name on them get thrown away. On the other hand, pens and pencils would stick around for a while. Every time a voter pulled my pen or pencil out, they'd see my name."

"Isn't this stuff expensive?" Lishia peered at the photos.

"It's an investment," Megan told her.

"An investment?" Janelle looked dubious.

"I read that things like this can help with college applications." Realizing it was past time to pick up Arianna, Megan started putting things back into her bag.

"But you were already accepted at your college," Lishia pointed out.

"I know." Megan stood. "But I haven't heard back on scholarships yet. If I win prom queen, it might help to secure some college money."

"That seems a little far-fetched," Janelle said. "But I vote for the candy. Even if they do throw away the wrapper, at least it might leave a good taste in their mouths." She laughed.

"Unless the chocolate's no good." Lishia tossed her empty coffee cup in the trash.

Note to self, Megan thought as they all went outside. *See if the candy company will send a sample of chocolate.*

six

Megan had only been eighteen for a couple months, but as she tapped into her college savings for prom queen expenses, she reminded herself that she was old enough to vote, which suggested that some considered her an adult. Convinced that she was in charge of her destiny and that these expenses were a solid investment in her future, she decided to order the Big Bonus Pack of chocolate bars.

Besides, she reminded herself as she typed her order, some of her college money was from past summer jobs. Really, it was her money. Right? However, when she hit "accept" on the charges being made to her bank account, she felt slightly guilty. Perhaps if Mom had been home, Megan might've asked for advice. But Mom always said, at least since the divorce, that her girls needed to be strong and independent and able to make smart decisions for themselves. Wasn't that precisely what Megan was doing?

While online, Megan decided to order some button-making

supplies, and eventually she began browsing prom dresses and shoes—just to get ideas, since she planned to go shopping in real stores once she lost a few pounds.

Of course, it wasn't until two hours later, when Mom came home from work with Chinese takeout for dinner, that Megan realized how much time had passed. She also realized that she still had unfinished homework to complete.

"What's your hurry?" Mom asked after Megan had wolfed down her chow mein and egg foo yong and excused herself.

"Homework," Megan explained as she put her plate in the dishwasher. Actually, she was relieved to get away before Mom or Arianna asked her how the prom queen campaign was going. She didn't want to have to tell them about her chocolate bar order, and she didn't want to lie. "Thanks for bringing home Chinese," she called as she headed back to her room.

❧

For the next several days, Megan felt like she was in prom queen campaign overdrive. So much needed to be done in order to get the fundraiser night on track. But at least Bethany Bridgewater had come through, confirming that her song and dance group was happy to perform if the date didn't conflict with another engagement. And then, after several tries, Megan was able to schedule the school cafeteria for her fundraiser—and it was on a night when Joyful Sound was available. So far so good.

"That's wonderful that you want to help the soup kitchen," Mrs. VanDrees told Megan after they secured the date. "It's refreshing to see students who are interested in helping others—simply for the satisfaction of giving."

Without going into all the details, Megan explained how she and her friends had volunteered at the soup kitchen. "It seemed like a lot of needy people really appreciated getting a hot meal."

"Well, I'm so impressed by your philanthropy that I'm going to ask my husband to provide a sculpture for your silent auction."

"A sculpture?"

Mrs. VanDrees jotted something on a notepad. "My husband is an artist. He works primarily in bronze. I'll see if he has something he wouldn't mind donating."

Megan thanked her, and then Mrs. VanDrees even offered to ask some of her other friends as well. Megan thanked her again. But as Megan walked to the library, she felt a conflicting mix of emotions. On one hand, she was pleased and proud at her success. On the other hand, she felt guilty. Mrs. VanDrees was completely unaware that Megan planned to run for prom queen. Would she suspect Megan's motives once she found out? Or shouldn't she be used to that sort of thing by now? After all, the school had lots of fundraisers with prizes attached. What was new about that?

Besides, Megan didn't have time to worry about that. Today was the first day of the book club she'd organized. It was her way of connecting with a new group of students. She'd put the announcement on the school's website last week, and to her surprise, nine students had responded. She had no idea what to expect but tried not to show her disappointment when she discovered a motley-looking group of somewhat mousy girls waiting for her to join them. Of course, she shouldn't have been too surprised that only female readers showed up (since her book choice was a recently released chick book), but these girls did not look like the kinds of students who could wield much influence in garnering votes for her election.

"Hi, I'm Megan Bernard," she said cheerfully as she sat down with her book in hand. She'd barely managed to finish it, and only after staying up past midnight, but at least it was still fresh in her mind. She started by asking the girls to introduce themselves. Most of them were younger than her, but, she reminded herself, a vote was a vote—and she was here to win theirs. She started out by talking about what she'd liked about the book, going on for several minutes. Then she paused to see if anyone else wanted to make a comment, but when no one said a word, she continued. This time she talked about what she did not like.

"Excuse me." An overweight girl named Brianna frowned at her. "Have you ever *led* a book group before?"

Megan laid her book in her lap. "Not really."

Now the other girls in the group exchanged glances. Almost like they knew something Megan did not.

"Do you even know *how* to lead a book group?" another girl asked.

Megan shrugged. "Don't we just talk about the book?"

"Yes . . . and no."

"Usually, *everyone* gets a chance to talk about the book," Brianna told her.

"Oh . . ." Megan nodded.

"Just because you're the leader doesn't mean you get to lecture us," someone else said.

"Uh, right." Megan made a forced smile. "I guess I was just waiting for you all to jump in."

Brianna held up her book, opening it to the back and pointing to a page. "Didn't you see the discussion questions?"

"Discussion questions?"

"Have you ever even been in a book group?" a brown-haired girl asked.

"Well, no, but I—"

"Then why did you offer to lead one?" the brown-haired girl demanded.

Megan didn't know what to say, but now others were expressing themselves, and all with one thing in mind—questioning why Megan felt qualified to do this.

"Give her a break," Brianna said finally.

"I'm sorry," Megan told them. "Maybe this was a bad idea. I just wanted to start a book group. I had no idea there were rules and—"

"It's not that there are rules," Brianna explained. "More like expectations."

Megan flipped to the back of her book now. "Should we go ahead and do the discussion questions?"

To her relief, the girls agreed this was a good plan. Then, one by one, they all took their time (lots and lots of time) to answer each one of the fifteen questions. Megan considered excusing herself before they were done, explaining she had to pick up her little sister, but instead she texted Arianna that she was running late. Fortunately, or unfortunately, Arianna texted back that she'd already gotten a ride home with a friend. It was after five by the time Megan finally peeled herself away from the book group. And only after they'd decided what next week's book would be. Of course, that meant that she was committed to show up here next Wednesday. Did these girls actually read a book a week?

As Megan drove home, she wondered how she could drop out of this pathetic little book group. However, she realized that a prom queen probably wouldn't do something like that. For now, she might as well go with the flow, maybe even fake that she'd read the upcoming book. Perhaps she could find something online to help her. Even so, it seemed like a lot of work for just nine measly votes . . . unless these girls became so loyal to her that they actually influenced their friends to vote for her too. That is, if they had friends.

Megan did a mental countdown of the time remaining until the prom queen election as she drove home. Four weeks. Most importantly, she had to get the fundraiser event solidly launched—this meant getting advertising and publicity started by the end of the week. And second most importantly, she had just one week to secure the nomination for prom queen. She knew she could count on her friends to nominate her, but it would take a few other nominations as well. Then the official campaigning would begin three weeks before the election.

She was just parking in front of the house when her cell phone rang. To her surprise it was Belinda. "Mom just told me the news," Belinda said in an unimpressed tone.

"The news?" Megan decided to play dumb.

"That you are actually going to make a run for the crown. Is it true?"

Megan removed her key from the ignition and stared up at the plastic gold heart that was still swaying back and forth, the tiny words "I Believe" barely readable.

"Well, is it?"

"Yeah." Megan grabbed her bag and got out of the car, holding her phone away from her ear as the loud shrieks of her older sister's laughter blasted through the phone. Megan was tempted to hang up as she went into the house.

"Are you still there?" Belinda demanded.

"What do you want?" Megan asked as she dumped her bag on her bed.

"I just wanted to know if it's really true." She chuckled.

"Yeah . . . I guess." Megan knew Pastor Robbie wouldn't approve of that response.

Belinda laughed loudly again. "I needed a little pick-me-up today, Meggie. Thanks for providing it!"

"Glad I could be of help!"

"Don't get mad at me, Megan. You're the one who needs to get her head examined."

"Thanks for the vote of confidence."

"Come on, Megan. You know this is totally crazy. Why on earth are you doing this?"

"It's not crazy." Megan sank down onto her desk chair, trying to remember words from *Shower of Power*.

"Listen, I'm your big sister, and I don't want to see you get hurt, okay?"

"I'm not going to get hurt."

"You *will* get hurt. Trust me—I know what I'm talking about. Running for prom queen is not for the faint of heart."

"My heart isn't faint."

"It's a brutal race, Megan. I know you. And you are simply not cut out for that kind of thing."

Megan let down her guard and actually told Belinda about

what she'd done so far. She explained how her friends were all helping, how she was planning a fundraiser, and how she had even started a book group.

"I already ordered chocolate bars with 'Vote for Megan Bernard' printed on the wrappers."

"Oh, Megan!" Belinda sounded truly concerned now.

"What?"

"They just say 'Vote for Megan Bernard'? That's all? You didn't even come up with a slogan first?"

"There was a limit on letters."

"Even so, you could've done better than 'Vote for Megan Bernard.' Good grief! Why didn't you check with me first?"

"I had to place the order if I wanted them to arrive in time for the election."

"But you should've used a slogan. Remember 'Believe in Belinda'? It was catchy and inspiring."

"Yeah, right." Megan kept her opinion to herself.

"Well, it helped win me the crown."

"Maybe so. But I haven't been able to come up with a slogan," Megan admitted.

"Let's see . . . how about 'Make It with Megan'?" She laughed. "No, that sounds a little disrespectable."

"Great, just what I need."

"Okay, what rhymes with Megan? How about 'Beggin' for Megan'?"

"No thanks."

"Well, I'll give it some thought. Now, you said you ordered candy bars, but did you already choose your campaign colors?"

"Campaign colors?" Megan sighed.

"You know, to coordinate everything. Remember, my colors were pink and black last year. I had them on my buttons and posters and everything. It was a very classic campaign."

Megan opened her laptop and pulled up one of the posters that Chelsea had made for her. "How about purple and teal?"

"*Purple and teal?* You've got to be kidding."

"A friend is helping with posters," she explained.

"But purple and teal?"

"That's just one of the layout choices."

"Why don't you email them to me? I'll look them over and come up with some suggestions."

Megan felt somewhat flattered by this unexpected interest and attention, but at the same time she felt slightly insulted too. Did Belinda really think Megan was incapable of running her own campaign?

"That is, unless you think you don't need my help . . ."

"No, no, I probably do need your help," Megan admitted. "I'll send the posters to you right now. I appreciate any recommendations you might have."

"See, already you're sounding more like a prom queen."

"I'm trying."

"And who knows, you just might be able to pull this off. I remember when I was a freshman and Patty Pringle was elected prom queen."

"Patty Pringle?"

"She was this loser chick, but she ran a really slick campaign and somehow she won." She giggled. "Of course, a bunch of kids boycotted prom that year. But it just goes to show you that anyone can win—if you just put your mind to it."

"Right." Megan wasn't sure whether to feel hopeful or hurt.

"I'm coming home this weekend," Belinda said. "Maybe I can spend some time coaching you."

"Okay." Megan brightened. "That would probably be helpful."

"In the meantime, don't make any more decisions. Not before we settle on a slogan and colors. Do you understand?"

Megan promised to put all decision-making on hold until Saturday. Feeling surprisingly encouraged, she hung up the phone and proceeded to email the posters to her sister. Really, with Belinda helping, she should be a shoo-in!

seven

By Saturday morning, Megan was ready to make some decisions—and she spent all day just waiting for Belinda to come home and help her. But so far, no big sister. As the day wore on, she left several texts and voice mail messages asking Belinda why she wasn't home yet. Consequently, when Belinda finally did come into the house, just as Megan was getting ready to go to youth group, it was not a pretty scene.

"Where have you been?" Megan demanded.

"I told you I was coming," Belinda tossed a bag of clothes into the laundry room.

"I waited all day for you!"

"Sorry, my ride couldn't leave until this afternoon." Belinda headed for the fridge. "But I'm here now."

"Yes, and I'm going to youth group."

Belinda turned and glared at her. "I came all this way to help you and you're leaving?"

"I spent all day just waiting for—"

"Girls!" Mom came into the kitchen waving her hands. "Can you keep it down? I'm working on a report and—" She noticed Belinda now, pausing to hug her. "Welcome home."

"Thanks. Now Megan tells me she's leaving." Belinda made a pouting face. "After I make all the effort to come and—"

"You could've told me when you'd get—"

"I have to rely on others for my rides these days." Belinda popped open a can of soda. "Unless you'd like to let me have my car back."

"We've been over that," Mom told her. "Now, really, can you keep it down so I can get some work done?"

"Fine, but now I think I wasted my time in coming."

"Can't we work on it tomorrow?" Megan asked.

"Celeste wants to head back to campus in the morning." Belinda set the can down with a loud clunk.

"Fine. I won't go to youth group tonight." Megan started to take off her jacket.

"Don't let me stop you."

Megan took a deep breath, reminding herself of how a prom queen should act. Too bad her sister wasn't setting a better example for her. "I'm sorry, Belinda," she said stiffly. "I'm glad you could come. And I do appreciate it. If tonight is all we have, we might as well get started."

"Speaking of getting started." Belinda nodded to the laundry room. "How about if you start a load for me while I go use the bathroom? It'll save time."

Controlling herself from complaining, Megan just nodded. Soon she was sorting Belinda's whites from colors, putting in a load, and realizing that running for prom queen came with all kinds of hidden costs.

"Come on into my room," Belinda called down the hallway. "And bring your laptop."

Soon they were both plunked in Belinda's pretty room, which was decorated in shabby chic pastels. Megan had always admired this space and had even asked about trading up after Belinda went off to college. Naturally, Belinda wouldn't hear of it. She insisted she needed a soft place to land during weekends at home.

"I think I've figured it out." Belinda was pulling up a formal dress website on Megan's computer. "We start with your dress and work backwards. I actually picked out my campaign colors first—pale pink and black—but that was okay since I wanted to go with a pink dress anyway. Fortunately, I look good in pale pink."

Megan sat down on Belinda's bed and just nodded as if she totally understood this.

"But with your coloring, I think you need a deeper color. No pastels for you." Belinda pointed to a hot pink dress. "What do you think of that?"

Megan shrugged. "It seems kind of bright."

"Yeah, maybe so."

"And I've never really been that into pink, you know?"

She nodded. "And the theme is Oscars Night, right?"

"The theme?"

"For prom." Belinda's brow creased. "Didn't you know that?"

"No." Megan frowned.

"Aren't you on the prom committee?"

Megan just shook her head.

Belinda looked truly stunned. "Then are you on a subcommittee?"

Again she shook her head.

"And you *are* running for prom queen?"

"Well, not officially. Nominations aren't until next week."

"You need to be on the committee, Megan." Belinda grabbed a pad of paper and began writing. "This is your new to-do list. First of all, get yourself on that prom committee. ASAP. You got that?"

"Okay."

"It's probably too late to get on the theme or set-up committee. One of the easiest committees is cleanup. It's easy because it doesn't require anything of you *before* prom—and that's when you're busiest. In the meantime, you can easily line up some friends to handle cleanup." She giggled. "You find some guy who's not exactly A-list, if you know what I mean. Make sure he likes you, and then very sweetly ask him to do you a big favor." She fluttered her eyelashes. "If he really likes you, he'll say yes. Then you explain what you need and ask him if he has some buddies who can help out." She grinned. "Easy breezy."

"Maybe for you." Megan bit her lip.

"Are you or are you not running for prom queen?"

"I am."

"Then start *thinking* like a prom queen."

Megan sat up straighter. "I've been trying to, Belinda. But you can be a little intimidating."

She simply smiled. "Get used to it, sweetheart. The girls running against you will be intimidating too. If you want to succeed, you can't let them get to you." She turned back to the laptop screen. "Now let's focus on colors. Since the theme is the Oscars, you want a sleek Hollywood sort of look. And

I assume you want a full-length dress. And even though there will probably be a red carpet, I don't think we should rule out red for your dress." She turned and peered at Megan. "You used to look pretty good in red."

"Used to?"

Belinda came over to look more closely, carefully examining Megan's hair. "You really should do something to perk up your color."

"Perk up my color?"

Belinda laughed. "I could swear there's an echo in this room."

"Excuse me for not understanding everything you say," Megan said defensively. "Maybe you could communicate a little more clearly."

"Okay, you need to see someone about intensifying your hair color. Right now it's kind of a drab brown. But you could get it highlighted or maybe even a red tone."

"But how? I don't know anything about hair coloring."

Belinda went back to her notepad. "I'll write down the name of my hairdresser for you. She's a pro at color."

"But I'm not a blonde."

Belinda rolled her eyes. "No one is asking you to be a blonde. I'm just saying do something with that dull brown hair. It should be shiny and vibrant. Anyway, back to dress colors. There are a lot of shades of red. But I think this one would be perfect for you." She pointed to a purplish shade of red. "Raspberry."

"Raspberry?"

"There's that echo again," Belinda teased. "And the only thing you can put with raspberries is chocolate."

Megan resisted the urge to echo that. Instead she just nodded. "That sounds tasty, but will it look okay?"

"If you do it right." Now Belinda pulled up one of the posters, pointing to where Chelsea had made borders of various colors. "Run the raspberry here, the chocolate there, and if you need a third color, I'd suggest a soft pink. But you'd probably be smart to keep it all to just the raspberry and chocolate." Now she asked Megan to show her where she'd ordered the chocolate bars. "So we can see if it's too late to change the wrapper."

Megan got back into the site, and then Belinda took over. "We'll see if your wrappers can be chocolate brown on the outside, like a Hershey's bar, and the lettering will be raspberry red and all caps. The words will say, 'Make It Megan!'— with an exclamation mark."

"Make It Megan!" She nodded eagerly. "I like that."

"So do I. Simple, but strong." Belinda finished up the message she was writing to the company, politely pleading for a change, then hit Send. Next she began focusing directly on Megan. "First you need to practice your posture," Belinda said. "Sitting, walking, standing. You realize you're a slumper, don't you?"

Megan shrugged.

"A slumper and a shrugger. Neither are particularly queenly traits." Now Belinda had Megan walk, stand, and sit with a book on her head. "You probably think this is silly, but if you could see how much prettier you look right now, you'd never slump again. Trust me."

As Megan practiced with the book on her head, she listened to Belinda espousing the benefits of good posture. She wanted to trust her sister. And really, why would Belinda lie to her about this sort of thing? Even so, she was glad her friends couldn't see her right now. She was also relieved that Arianna was at a sleepover tonight.

"Now let's work on your makeup and beauty routines." Belinda chuckled as she led Megan to the bathroom. "This is something I've wanted to do to you for years."

Megan knew that Belinda had always spent much longer getting ready for school than Megan. But because the three girls shared the bathroom, the time that Belinda used had always cut into Megan and Arianna's turns. As a result, Megan had learned to be very quick in getting ready. In fact, until recently, she'd taken pride in being such a low-maintenance sort of girl. Of course, those days were gone now.

As Belinda explained some of the basics of skin care and makeup, retrieving some of her own left-behind beauty products from a drawer in the vanity, Megan told her about the makeover and photo shoot they'd done last weekend.

"I thought you looked extra good on those posters," Belinda said as she showed Megan how to apply eyeliner. "The thing is, you need to look like that *every* day."

"Every day?"

"Every day that you're running for prom queen." Now Belinda showed her the proper use of concealer. "There really is an art form to hiding zits," she explained as she first applied a tiny dot of concealer, then patted some powder on over it, then lightly brushed it off with a big fluffy brush from Belinda's own cosmetic bag. "I'll help you to find the tools and products you need online," she promised. "There's a really good site where I get all my stuff." Next she showed

Megan how to use lip liner, lipstick, and finally lip gloss to make her lips appear fuller.

"Wow." Megan peered at her own image. "You really do know what you're doing."

"That's what I've been trying to tell you for years. You just wouldn't listen."

"I'm listening now."

Belinda went over some more things, including going through Megan's closet and tossing out what looked like nearly half of Megan's clothes. "And don't you dare give those things to Arianna either," Belinda warned.

Megan laughed. "Don't worry. Arianna wouldn't want them."

"Now let's go back to my closet. Even my castoff clothes are better than most of the things you've been wearing."

Megan tried not to be offended. "You know, Belinda," she said calmly as Belinda began handing her items of clothing. "I think I've spent more time on my inner self than I have on my outer self. I used to think that was good."

"It's good if you want to become a nun." Belinda laughed.

With an armload of clothes and a whole lot more of Belinda's wardrobe advice, Megan suddenly found herself feeling overwhelmed. More than ever, she wished she were at youth group tonight. At youth group, she usually ended up feeling better about herself. Right now she felt blurry and buried—and not just in clothes either.

"Maybe I'm in over my head," she confessed as they were sorting and hanging the clothes in Megan's reorganized closet. "You told me before that I wasn't the prom queen type. Maybe I really am delusional."

Belinda firmly shook her head. "No, after spending time with you tonight, I honestly think you can do this, Megan."

"Really?"

Belinda put a hand on her shoulder. "I do. You're changing. I think if you keep working at this, if you really set your heart on achieving it and keep thinking positively, you can do this."

"It's a lot of work."

"I know."

They spent the rest of the evening looking at dresses, shoes, and hairstyles online. Belinda was slowly getting the choices narrowed down, and her plan was for the two of them to go shopping next weekend.

"But what about my weight?" Megan asked. "I wanted to lose at least five pounds by prom."

"If we find a dress, and that's a big if, we'll make sure it's a little on the snug side. If you lose more than five pounds, which would be great, you can always have it taken in."

"*More* than five pounds?" Megan knew she'd be lucky to lose five.

Belinda pulled up a website with the latest diet plan. "If you follow this, you could easily lose ten pounds by prom," she assured her.

"I'll print it out," Megan told her. "Thanks."

It was late by the time Megan went to bed, but she knew that it had been time well spent. She hadn't been very close to Belinda. Not since they were little girls, playing with Barbies. And never in her life had Megan felt so truly thankful for her older sister's help. Tonight she realized that Belinda really was one in a million, and not only did Megan feel blessed to have such a sister—she did not want to let her down!

eight

Megan had heard it said that it took two weeks to change a habit, but two weeks after her decision to run for prom queen, she felt like a totally new person. And she wasn't the only one to notice the change.

"Something about you is different."

Megan was surprised to see Jack Speers in the lunch line behind her. She had known Jack for several years. Like her, he was in choir, but unlike her, he was known as a singing sensation. He had a baritone voice that landed him the best solos in choral concerts. But right now, Jack was staring at her—almost as if seeing her for the first time.

"Did you say something to me?" Megan asked him.

He twisted his mouth to one side. "I can't put my finger on it, but I've noticed it lately. Something about you is different."

"Different good? Or different bad?" She removed a straw from the dispenser.

He grinned. "Different *good*."

"Thanks. I'll take that as a compliment."

"It is a compliment."

"Are you trying out for the spring musical?" she asked as she moved forward in the line. It was the only small talk she could think of, but she wanted to keep this conversation going.

"I wasn't really planning on it, but everyone's been nagging me. And this is my last year, so I suppose I should." He set a napkin on his tray. "How about you?"

"Oh, I don't know." Megan hadn't been in a musical since her sophomore year.

"Oh, come on," he urged her. "You'd look great in a babushka."

She laughed. "So it's decided then? They're really doing *Fiddler on the Roof?*"

He rubbed his chin. "Yeah, already I'm starting to itch."

"Huh?"

"You know, the glue for sticking on the beards. I'll bet it's itchy."

"Does that mean you'd play the father? I can't remember the name."

"Tevye," he offered. "Yeah, that's probably the role I'd go for. He gets some great songs. But I think most of the guys will have to wear beards."

It was almost her turn at the register. "Well, I'm sure you'd be a good Tevye," she said over her shoulder.

"Hey, why don't you try out for Golde?" He leaned forward and spoke quietly in her ear as she dug out her cash. *"That's Tevye's wife."*

She felt a warm rush of delight as she looked into his dark

brown eyes. "Is that a come-on line?" she asked in a slightly teasing tone.

He chuckled. "Maybe so."

She giggled as she handed the cashier a five.

"So you'll think about it?"

She looked back at him and smiled. "Golde, eh?"

His eyes twinkled. "Tryouts start after school on Thursday."

She moved away from the register so he could pay for his lunch but lingered nearby to finish the conversation.

"So, whaddya think?" he asked as he joined her.

"I think I might do it," she said shyly. "But only if you promise to try out with me."

He nodded eagerly. "Okay then, it's a deal."

He walked with her to the table where her friends were already seated, and she asked him if he wanted to join them. To her surprise, he actually seemed to consider it, but then he nodded over to where some of his music friends were waiting. "Not this time, but I'm serious about tryouts. Let's do it together—like a package deal. It'll be fun."

She felt herself being swept away by his charm as she agreed.

"Great! I'll catch you after lunch and we can put together a plan," he told her.

"Sounds good." She sat down with her friends, trying not to giggle.

"What is going on between you and Jack Speers?" Lishia asked with wide-eyed interest.

"I'm not totally sure," Megan quietly confessed, "but I think he's coming on to me." She told them about Jack's suggestion that they try out for the musical together. "I told him I'd do it!" Now she did break out into giggles. "Can you believe that? Jack and me playing husband and wife in *Fiddler*?"

"You don't have time to be in a musical this year," Janelle told her. "You've already got the fundraiser and your book club, not to mention your campaign—that is, unless you plan to give up running for prom queen."

"She can't give that up," Chelsea said quickly. "She's already ordered her posters and flyers and candy and stuff."

"Don't worry," Megan assured them. "I'm not giving anything up. I'll just humor Jack and see where it goes. Besides, if I can get Jack's support, that could mean a lot of votes from his friends too."

"And everyone knows Jack Speers has lots of friends." Lishia nodded over to the table where Jack was surrounded by a small crowd of girls and fellow music kids.

"Hey, does Jack have a girlfriend?" Chelsea asked. "If not, maybe he could be Megan's date for the prom."

Janelle and Lishia found this highly amusing. Megan knew this was because despite being constantly surrounded by admiring girls, Jack Speers never seemed to have a girlfriend.

"Rumor has it that Jack isn't into girls," Janelle told Chelsea. "I mean, as far as dating, if you know what I mean." She chuckled like this was really funny.

"You shouldn't repeat things you don't know for sure," Megan sternly told her. "That's like gossiping. And you know that's wrong, Janelle."

Janelle held up her hands. "Just saying."

"Well, don't!" Megan glared at her.

"Sorry." Janelle rolled her eyes. "You don't have to go ballistic."

After lunch, Megan joined Jack in the courtyard, where they made a quick plan to meet after school, get some scripts, and practice a scene together. Megan knew she might be putting too much on her plate, but she didn't care. If anyone had told her just a few weeks ago that she would be trying out for the spring musical with the delectable Jack Speers, she would not have believed it. It was like her life and high school experience were finally turning into what she'd always dreamed they should be, and she had to think it was all due to Pastor Robbie's *Shower of Power* sermon about positive thinking. Maybe she should write him a thank-you letter.

Another interesting development in Megan's amazing new life was that Dayton Moore (star quarterback and Kingston hottie) seemed to be growing increasingly interested in her. At first she'd assumed he only wanted her academic assistance. But after she helped him with his essay, he continued trailing her, and Megan realized that for the first time in her life, she was actually flirting. And it felt great!

"Want to go grab something to eat with me?" he asked her after school.

"You mean right now?" She closed her locker and studied him.

"Yeah, I'm starving."

She laughed. "Thanks, but I have to meet someone."

He frowned. "What about later?"

She explained her plan to try out with Jack for the musical.

Dayton made a crooked smile. "Well, I guess I don't need to be too worried then."

"Huh?"

"I mean 'cause it's just Jack. It's not like he's real competition."

Megan's smile faded.

Dayton patted her on the cheek. "You're sweet," he said in a patronizing way. "Catch ya later."

She just nodded as she called Arianna's number, explaining that she was going to be running late again.

"More prom queen stuff?" Arianna asked.

Megan told her about the musical.

"Really, you're going to be in *Fiddler on the Roof*?" Arianna actually sounded impressed. "That's so cool."

"Nothing is for sure yet," Megan explained. "Tryouts aren't until Thursday. But I promised to practice with a friend today. Probably tomorrow too."

"I'll just plan to ride home with Olivia this week," Arianna offered.

Megan thanked her and headed off toward the music department, but on her way, she noticed Zoë again. Determined not to make the same overly friendly mistake as before, Megan considered taking a different route, except that she was already running late. Zoë was with a guy today, so Megan decided to give them plenty of space. Keeping her eyes off them, she cut a wide berth, attempting to hurry past.

"Ouch!" Zoë shrieked. "Knock it off, Trevor!"

Megan heard the guy curse, followed by what sounded like a loud smack. Despite wanting to ignore whatever was going on, Megan stopped and turned to see. Zoë's hand was on her face, and she had a hurt look in her eyes. Had he hit her?

"I said knock it off," Zoë told Trevor. But instead of backing off, he grabbed her arm, twisted it behind her, made a fist, and looked like he was about to punch her in the face.

"Hey!" Megan yelled. "Zoë said to knock it off."

"Butt out, you—"

"Go away!" Zoë warned Megan.

"No." Megan reached into her bag, pulled out her phone, and held it up like a weapon. "If you don't leave Zoë alone, I'm calling 911. Right now."

Now he swore at her.

"I mean it," she yelled loudly, hoping that someone would hear her and come over to help, or at least witness what was escalating into a frightening scene. "Leave her alone!"

Trevor released Zoë's arm, but now he came directly toward Megan.

"Back off!" Megan yelled as she focused on her phone, punching the nine with a shaky finger.

"Don't touch her!" Zoë yelled.

Just then Megan's phone was whacked from her hand. She looked up in time to see Trevor about to smack her, but in that same instant Zoë swung her backpack like a club, landing it solidly across the side of his head. He reeled off to one side, and Megan dove to get her phone, which had snapped in two.

"This time I mean it," she yelled as she held her broken phone as if it was still working. "I'm calling 911 right now!"

Trevor glared at her, then swore at Zoë, but to Megan's relief he took off running.

"Are you okay?" she asked Zoë.

"Are you really calling 911?" Zoë came over to see.

Megan held up her ruined phone.

"Sorry about that," Zoë said.

"What was that all about?" Megan studied the bright red mark on Zoë's cheek. "Why was he hitting you?"

"Trevor's a jerk."

"A nasty, mean, bully sort of a jerk." Megan dropped the remains of her phone into her bag. "But seriously, why was he hitting you?"

"It's a long story."

"Are you guys a couple?"

"Not anymore." Zoë let out a weary sigh. "That's why he was so mad. I just broke up with him."

"Good for you."

Zoë shrugged.

"Seriously, Zoë." Megan peered into her eyes. "You could do a lot better than someone like that."

"Trevor wasn't always that way. He was nice when we first got together."

"I don't recall seeing him before. Does he actually go to school here?"

Zoë shook her head.

"Then he shouldn't even be on campus."

"It's no big deal."

Megan put her hand on Zoë's shoulder. "It is a big deal. That guy is a brute. He hit you, and it looked like he wasn't finished either." Megan frowned. "Are you even safe now?"

Zoë looked like she was about to cry.

"Look, I've got to meet somebody, but you could come with me. Then I can give you a ride home afterwards. Okay?"

Zoë seemed uncertain.

"Come on," Megan urged her. "I'm already running late." Then to Megan's relief, Zoë walked with her. As they headed for the music building, Megan explained who she was meeting and why. Zoë didn't say anything, but at least she came along.

Zoë sat in the back of the room while Jack and Megan practiced some lines and then sang "Sunrise, Sunset" a couple of times. Megan was having such a good time that she almost forgot about Zoë and the earlier altercation, but when they finally finished up, Zoë was still waiting, reading a paperback book. She didn't even seem very perturbed that it had taken nearly two hours.

"That was awesome," Jack told her. "You'll make a great Golde."

"Your voice is perfect for Tevye," she said.

"You guys sounded pretty good together." Zoë shoved the book in her pack. Megan had briefly explained to Jack about the episode with Trevor. Thankfully, he wasn't asking too many questions.

"Same time, same place tomorrow?" Jack asked.

"Sure." Megan nodded as she picked up her bag.

As Megan and Zoë walked to the parking lot, Megan kept glancing around, trying to make sure that Trevor wasn't lurking somewhere, ready to jump them. Finally they were safe in her car and she started to relax. "How are you doing?" she asked Zoë as she pulled out onto the street.

"I'm fine."

"Do you think Trevor will leave you alone now?"

Zoë just shrugged.

"Do you still live in Tuscan Heights?"

She nodded. "Why are you being nice to me, Megan?"

Megan wasn't sure how to answer. "We used to be friends, remember?"

"Yeah, but then you ditched me in middle school."

Megan glanced at her. "I ditched you?"

Zoë nodded, slumping down into the seat in a dejected way.

"I didn't ditch you, Zoë. You started getting wild and running around with kids who were trouble—kids like Trevor."

"That's because you ditched me."

Megan felt confused. "No," she insisted. "You ditched me."

"Seriously?" Zoë frowned. "You honestly think I ditched you?"

Megan firmly nodded. "I know you did. I remember when I told you that I couldn't be friends with Devin Gartolli. I knew she was into drugs and alcohol and I just didn't want to go there. But you insisted on hanging with her. It was like you chose her over me. Don't you remember that?"

"Maybe it was a mutual ditching," she conceded.

"Can I ask you something?" Megan turned into Zoë's subdivision.

"I guess."

"Are you glad you made the choices you did?"

Zoë laughed, but there was a lot of sadness in it.

"I mean, if you could do it over, would you do it all the same way?"

"Obviously I'd do some things differently." Zoë pulled her backpack onto her lap and removed a package of cigarettes, shaking one out.

Megan didn't want her to smoke in the car, but Zoë's house was only a few blocks away, so she didn't say anything as Zoë lit up, although she did put her window down. "Well, maybe we can be friends now," Megan said as she pulled in front of Zoë's house. It looked a lot more run down than it used to.

"Yeah, right. I'm sure we're going to be best friends now." Zoë opened the door and stuck a foot out.

"Fine, maybe we won't be best friends." Megan gave her a wistful smile. "But at least we can say hi and stuff, can't we?"

"Sure. Why not?" Zoë climbed out.

"Take care."

Zoë leaned down with a sad little smile. "Thanks for helping me."

Megan just nodded and waved as Zoë closed the door. As she drove home, she wished she'd said something more to her. Maybe she should've invited Zoë to come to youth group on Saturday. Or maybe that was pushing too hard. The important thing was that it seemed like she'd made a real connection with her old friend. And it seemed like Zoë had appreciated it. That felt amazingly good.

nine

The first good news Megan heard on Friday was that she was "official." Thanks to several of her friends, she'd been nominated as a candidate for prom queen.

"Congratulations," Lishia told her as the four friends met at lunch.

"Thanks." Megan nodded humbly. "I'll do my best to make you guys proud."

"Well, it must be a relief." Janelle picked up a tray. "After all you've invested in it already." She nodded to Chelsea. "And you can thank her for getting you nominated."

"Really, did you—"

"I just mentioned to several people on the nominating committee that you would make a wonderful prom queen," Chelsea told her. "I guess they listened."

"Unfortunately, your competition is stiff," Lishia pointed out.

"No surprises there," Megan admitted. "Amanda and Hallie."

"But maybe you're right about them," Chelsea reminded her. "You know, your theory about splitting the popular vote. That could work to your benefit."

"I sure hope so." Megan put a cap on her diet soda, trying not to reveal how scary this was becoming. What if she was in over her head? Would she end up looking like a complete fool? But instead of obsessing, she reminded herself of Pastor Robbie's words, and remembering her sister's advice, she held her head high.

At the end of the day, Megan heard more good news— she'd gotten the part of Golde in the musical. She wasn't sure if it was because of her own audition or because of her relationship with Jack, but she didn't really care either. To be participating in a show, singing with friends, and just being with Jack was an unexpected dream for her. All in all, it had been a very encouraging day!

However, she was aware that this new commitment might make her campaign for prom queen a bit more challenging. Some might even consider the musical a distraction, but she truly believed she was up for it. And, she told herself, being in the musical was a way to be in the spotlight, to make friends, and hopefully to gain votes. Really, it sounded like a win-win-win to her.

"Just because you *can* doesn't mean you *should*," Janelle warned her after hearing the news about Megan's role in *Fiddler*. The four friends were spending their Friday evening on the hunt for prom dresses, but so far no actual purchases had been made.

"That's right," Lishia agreed. She turned to look at her image in the three-way mirror. The shiny black dress she was trying on reminded Megan of an elongated black garbage bag.

"You're stretching yourself too thin," Janelle called over the changing room door.

"I wish it would make me thin." Megan poked her midsection, which was bulging through the thin fabric of the slinky magenta dress she had on.

"I think it's great you're doing the musical," Chelsea said as she came out wearing a shiny pale blue dress. "I mean, if that's what you want. The prom shouldn't take over your entire life."

"But what about the fundraiser?" Lishia asked. "We still have so much work to do. How is Megan going to help with that?"

"By delegating," Chelsea said. "We just need to round up some more volunteers."

"What do you think of this one?" Janelle emerged in a raspberry red gown.

"Hey, where did you find that?" Megan asked.

"Out there." Janelle turned to check out the back. "I kinda like it."

"But that's the color *I'm* supposed to wear," Megan told her.

Janelle frowned. "You mean you're going to dictate what we can and cannot wear to prom?"

"No, but you knew that was the color I was going for. It's on my posters and buttons and everything."

"Well, it's not your size." Janelle did a little twirl, making the skirt flare out. "So it's a moot point."

"It's not a moot point," Megan told her. "Because if I find a dress in my size and in that color, I'm getting it."

"So?" Janelle put her hands on her hips.

"So we'll look like twins."

"Are you saying I can't get this dress?" Janelle looked angry now. "It's the first one I've actually liked, and it fits me perfectly."

Megan looked to Lishia to back her, but Lishia just shrugged and disappeared back into her changing room. Now Megan looked hopefully at Chelsea.

"Megan did say she wanted a dress in that color," Chelsea reminded Janelle. "It seems a little mean-spirited that you're suddenly glomming onto it too. Besides, you said you were going to get an orange dress. And you do look great in orange."

"I can't find an orange dress," Janelle complained. "What's wrong with this?"

Megan made an exasperated sigh.

"Why can't you wear that one?" Janelle pointed at Megan. "That color's not so different than this." She stood beside Megan now. "They even kind of go together."

"For starters, this dress doesn't even fit me. Besides that, I look terrible in this scoop neckline. And finally, it's the wrong color." She almost added that it also wasn't fair that Janelle, who wasn't even running for prom queen, looked way better than Megan did, but that would sound too whiny.

"Seriously, Megan." Janelle held up her hands. "You're starting to remind me of Bridezilla. Only we'd have to call you *Queenzilla*." She laughed as she returned to her changing room.

"Real nice," Megan said as the door slammed shut. She looked at Chelsea now. "Am I being unfair?"

Chelsea shrugged. "Maybe it was a bad idea to go dress shopping as a group."

"I thought it would be fun if our dresses went together," Megan protested. "Then when we get photos taken, we'll all look good."

"It sounded like a fun idea. But maybe we all just need to focus on getting our own dresses."

Megan nodded. "I guess so. My sister wanted to help me do some online shopping tomorrow anyway. I suppose I should wait and see what she has in mind."

Megan returned to her dressing room, ready to give up, but then she decided to try one last gown. This one was a sleeveless plum number with a beaded V neckline. Very sophisticated. But once again, it was too tight. Her girls looked like they wanted to bust out and make a run for it. Yet the cut of the dress was actually flattering. She went back out to the open area to get a better look at the dress.

Naturally, with the extra light and huge three-way mirrors, the dress looked even worse than she'd imagined. "Nothing looks good on me," she complained hopelessly.

Now Lishia came out wearing a creamy white satin dress which was actually pretty fabulous. Lishia frowned at Megan. "That one's too small too, Megan. Why don't you try the next size up, or maybe even two sizes?"

"Because I'm trying to lose weight," she said with irritation. "I already told you that."

Chelsea came out in a halter style silver gown. She too looked stunning. But then all the dresses looked good on Chelsea. She just had one of those bodies that made everything look great. "Lishia's right, Megan. You should try something in your own size. Then if you do lose the weight, you can have it taken in—in the right spots."

"Or else you can wear Spanx underneath," Janelle told her as she came out wearing a bright yellow dress. "That's what my mom does." Janelle looked at her own reflection and groaned. "This color makes me look like I'm seriously ill."

Chelsea chuckled. "It's pretty bad, Janelle."

Janelle pointed her finger at Megan. "It's your fault. If you'd let me get that raspberry gown like I wanted—"

"Go ahead and get it," Megan told her as she turned back to her dressing room. She felt tears filling her eyes, and she didn't want her friends to see her like this. This was not how a prom queen should be acting.

"I have an idea," Chelsea called out. "Let Janelle try on those gowns that were too small for you, Megan. They're probably Janelle's size anyway. And we know those colors look good with the raspberry. Plus they should look good on Janelle."

"Fine." Megan gathered up the dresses in her arms, and wearing only her underwear, she carried them out and foisted them onto Janelle. "Happy now?"

Janelle laughed, pointing at Megan's backside. "Do you know you've got a hole in your panties?" Of course, this made the other girls laugh too. Suddenly they were all teasing the prom queen about her holey undies.

"You're all just plain mean," Megan muttered as she hurried back to her changing room. This time she put her street clothes back on. She was finished with dress shopping. She wanted to be finished with her friends too. Well, except for Chelsea. She seemed to be the only nice one in the bunch.

"I know what's wrong with us," Chelsea said. "We're all hungry. It was a bad idea to shop on empty stomachs."

"It was Megan's idea," Janelle called out.

"Fine, blame it all on me." Megan came out, flopping down on the chaise next to the mirrors. "I'm a big girl. I can take it."

They asked the salesgirl to hold their favorite dresses, then headed off to the food court to forage. However, as Megan surveyed the menu boards, she realized that most of the choices were high in calories and fat. And her Laguna Light diet strictly ruled out most of them. She walked around and around, trying to find something not in conflict with her diet. Finally, out of desperation, she decided on a large garden salad with lemon juice. She carried that and a Diet Coke back to where her friends were already porking out on pizza and other greasy items that looked delicious—and fattening.

"Poor Megan," Lishia pointed to the bowl of greens. "That is so sad."

"Three weeks from now, it won't be sad," Megan said with determination as she forked her salad.

"Speaking of deadlines—the fundraiser is less than two weeks out now." Chelsea twisted a stringy piece of cheese around her finger and popped it into her mouth. "Let's go over some of the details for that, okay?"

"Good idea." Lishia nodded. "The bowl project is coming along nicely. But as we get closer to the date, we could use some help with glazing. The plan is to have a big stockpile of about a hundred bowls."

"Is that enough?" Megan asked. "What if more than a hundred people come?"

"We'll have a backup of other bowls," Chelsea explained. "And there'll be enough soup for at least three hundred people."

"And it's still going to be stone soup?" Megan asked. "Where everyone brings the ingredients?"

"Kind of, but with a slight revision," Chelsea told her. "I was talking to Marie, the head cook, and she came up with a good suggestion. We'll go ahead and have people bring the food items—just like it says on the posters and advertisements—and we'll use some of the things they bring. But Marie offered to help us create three different kinds of soups based on different stocks. That way there should be something for everyone. And then any food items we have left over, as well as any soup, will be donated to the soup kitchen."

"Good idea," Megan said as she chewed her salad. The idea of a tasty bowl of soup made her even hungrier.

"It's brilliant," Janelle added. "In fact, I'll tell my aunt to adapt the radio ad to explain that. It will show people that we're really thinking."

"Now, I want to go over the silent auction items." Chelsea pulled a notebook from her bag and started telling them about who was donating what and who they still needed to approach. "My stepmom offered to take me around to pick up the items. We'll do it on Tuesday, the day before the auction," she explained. "But it would be nice to have some help setting up the items on Wednesday afternoon, before the dinner. We need to get them all numbered and the silent auction forms laid out with pens and stuff. I'm guessing it could take a couple of hours."

"I'll be busy getting the bowls from the art room to the cafeteria," Lishia said. "They need to go through the dishwasher too. Then I want to set them up to look like an art exhibit."

"And I'm going to be collecting the desserts and getting that all set up." Janelle pointed her fork at Megan. "What are you doing, anyway?"

Megan shrugged. "Whatever you guys want me to do."

There was a quiet pause at the table, and for some reason Megan felt defensive. "I secured the location for the fundraiser," she said, "and I've helped put up posters and stuff."

"So you'll help getting the auction items all set up then?" Chelsea asked her.

"Sure. You just tell me what to do and I'll be happy to do it." Megan forced a smile. Was it just her imagination, or were her friends treating her differently?

Before long they returned to dress shopping, and although Megan tried on the right-sized gowns this time, she still never found anything that she absolutely loved. Nothing that cried out "prom queen." In fact, it seemed the more she looked, the more discouraged she felt.

"It's hopeless," she said as they waited for Janelle to finish her purchase. She'd finally decided on the plum gown with the beaded V neckline that Megan had considered. "I can't believe I'm the only one who didn't find a dress."

"Belinda will help you figure it out," Lishia assured her.

"I love the gown you got," Megan told her.

"But you said it looked like a wedding gown," Lishia reminded her.

"I was probably just jealous." Megan turned to Chelsea. "And that silver halter dress looks fantastic on you. Good choice."

"I can't wait to see what you pick out," Chelsea told her. "Remember to email us the photo when you find it."

"Ready to look for shoes?" Janelle asked as she rejoined them.

"Shop till we drop," Chelsea said. "But if we want to save some bucks, I suggest we head over to Best 4 Less. Kate just told me about a new shipment of designer shoes that arrived this week. She said there are some real gems in the mix."

"What about you, Megan?" Lishia asked as they loaded their things in the back of Megan's car. "Can you look for shoes if you don't have a dress?"

"I can look." Megan got into the driver's seat.

"If you find a pair that you love, you could always get them tonight and hope they go with your dress," Chelsea suggested. "And return them if they don't."

Megan shook her head as she started the engine. In some ways it felt like she was doing this all backwards. "What if I end up with great shoes and no dress?"

"Just make sure you don't wear your holey undies," Janelle teased.

Megan laughed. "Can you imagine being crowned prom queen in your underwear? Sounds like a bad dream. But if I'm worried about not having a dress yet, I suppose I should be even more worried about not having a date. At least I'm not the only one." She nudged Lishia with her elbow.

"Didn't you tell Megan?" Janelle asked from the backseat.

"Tell me what?"

"I'm going to prom with Anders," Lishia said. "I thought I already told you."

"Anders from art?"

"Yeah." Lishia giggled. "He's been helping me with the bowl project, and I explained about how it all started when you decided to run for prom queen, then I confessed that I didn't even have a date for the prom . . . like hint, hint . . . and the next thing I knew he was asking me to go with him. Can you believe it?"

"That's great news." Megan tried to sound more enthused than she felt. "Everyone has a date now . . . except for me."

"You'd better work on that," Janelle told her. "Chase told me that guys need to be reserving their tuxes at least two weeks before prom. And they get better choices if they reserve them earlier."

"Nicholas is using an old tux from the sixties," Chelsea told them. "I guess his mom found it on eBay or somewhere, but it sounds pretty cool."

Megan tried not to be jealous, but by the time they were trying on shoes, she felt pea green with envy. Not only did her friends have dates and dresses, but by the end of the evening, they had very cool shoes too.

"Are you sure you don't want to get those silver shoes?" Chelsea asked Megan as they were waiting in line. "They'd go with almost anything, and I think they'd look great with raspberry."

"I don't know." Megan frowned. "I need to hear what Belinda has to say." The truth was, Megan felt completely confused now. She had no idea what kind of dress she would be wearing or what kind of shoes would go with it. By the time she got home, she was actually beginning to doubt the whole thing. Maybe her silly dream of becoming prom queen was just that—a silly dream!

ten

W hat do you mean you're not going with us?" Lishia demanded on the phone Saturday morning. "We're doing this fundraiser for you, Megan. Volunteering at the soup kitchen was supposed to be part of the plan. Besides that, we were going to tell Bertie and the others about it today. Don't you want to make that announcement?"

Megan switched her recently replaced cell phone to the other ear. "I can't, Lishia. Belinda is coming home today—she already told me it was inconvenient and she's coming just to help me. I can't take off and not even be here."

"Whatever." Her tone was full of exasperation. "Although I don't see how you can feel very good about calling this *your* fundraiser. It seems like everyone else is working on it except you."

"It was *my* idea," Megan protested.

"Actually the Stone Soup Silent Auction was Chelsea's idea."

"You know what I mean."

"Yeah, I know . . . I gotta go."

Megan felt guilty as she closed her phone. But it was true. Belinda *was* coming to help her today, although she hadn't said what time she'd actually get here. But besides that, Megan had asked Arianna and Olivia to start making the campaign buttons today. She needed to be around to keep them on task as well as to order them pizza and things.

Megan's plan was to hang posters and start handing out buttons first thing on Monday. That was the official start of the prom queen campaign, and she planned to make the most of every moment before the election. That meant she had this weekend to get everything ready. She also needed to find the perfect gown, and maybe the shoes and accessories as well. She was determined not to let this weekend pass without bagging that dress. She knew that Belinda would back her in this pursuit.

However, as Megan sat by herself in the kitchen, tediously cutting out dozens of button-sized circles with her name and slogan printed on them, she could feel her enthusiasm waning. If there was a way to bow out of this thing gracefully, she would probably seriously consider it. But how could she put on the brakes without looking totally foolish to her friends and family? And what about all she'd invested already? She set another paper circle in the basket and sighed. No, she needed to see this through to completion. And perhaps when that moment came—when the crown was placed upon her head—she would be grateful for the sacrifices she had made in order to gain it.

"The official campaign starts on Monday," she told Belinda when she arrived in midafternoon. "There's a lot to get done in a short amount of time." This time Megan was careful not to complain about Belinda's lateness, but she realized she could've gone to the soup kitchen after all. She wondered if she hadn't really been using Belinda as an excuse, just because it had been so uncomfortable the last time. But these were thoughts she shoved down deep . . . along with all the other naysayers' doubts.

"Believe me, I know." Belinda slumped down onto her bed with a sigh. "But first of all I need a little nap. Okay?"

Megan blinked. "A nap?"

"I had a late night last night. And college is hard, Megan. Weekends are my only chance to catch up on my beauty sleep."

"But what about—"

"Trust me, I'll be much more useful to you *after* I get some shut-eye." Belinda held a forefinger to her lips. "Just twenty minutes or so."

Twenty minutes turned into two hours. However, Megan managed to stay busy by working with Arianna and Olivia. Still, making buttons and flyers and posters was feeling tedious, and by five o'clock, shortly before Belinda woke up, the girls were demanding pizza and videos again.

"Get enough for me too," Belinda called as Megan was leaving. "But we'd better not catch you sneaking any, Megan."

Well, Megan did sneak some as she drove home. She couldn't help herself—she was starving. She tried to rearrange the pizza so it wouldn't show, but Belinda wasn't fooled.

"Do you or do you not want to become prom queen?" she

demanded as she took a large piece, wrapping the cheese around her finger.

"I do. And I've been really good on the diet too." Megan went to get a diet soda. "I just couldn't bear smelling that pepperoni."

"Well, get down on the floor and do some push-ups and sit-ups. About fifty of each. That should help."

The last thing Megan wanted to do was push-ups and sit-ups, especially while everyone else was snarfing down pizza. But she could tell that Belinda wasn't kidding, so she complied. Or at least pretended to.

"Now it's time to do some serious dress shopping," Belinda announced as she tossed the empty pizza box into the fireplace. "Bring your laptop down here."

Before long, Belinda was perusing BlueFly, flipping through dress after dress until she found it. "This is the right one." She clicked to enlarge the photo, and Megan stared at a long, shiny, raspberry-colored gown.

"Is that satin?" Megan asked.

"Yes." Belinda pointed to the bodice. "See the way the fabric is draped to fold across the bustline like this? Very flattering."

"Ooh, that's pretty," Arianna cooed.

"Really sophisticated," Olivia confirmed.

"But will it look good on me?" Megan demanded. "I tried on a whole bunch and they all looked lousy and—"

"Trust me," Belinda told her. "This design is foolproof. Anyone can wear it and look fantastic. Besides that, it's a Nicole Miller—known for quality and style—and it's a classic. And isn't the color perfect?"

"I guess." Megan was trying to imagine how it would look on her. "After trying on some sleeveless dresses, I wasn't too sure it was such a good—"

"Of course you're going sleeveless, Megan. Honestly, you didn't think you were going to wear sleeves to prom?"

Megan flexed a bicep. "It's just that my arms are, well, a little chubby."

Arianna giggled.

"Come on," Olivia urged. "Let's stay out of this."

Belinda reached over to feel Megan's bicep. "Well, you just need to start doing some exercises. Then we'll get you a good fake tan. That always makes you look slimmer. No problem."

Megan studied the dress more carefully. "It is pretty." And it did look good on the model—but she was a model.

"What size are you wearing?"

"I'm not really sure," Megan admitted. "When I tried on dresses, they all seemed to be different."

"Then we'll do it the old-fashioned way." Belinda went over to the junk drawer and removed a measuring tape.

Megan cringed.

"Come on over here." Belinda remained in the kitchen. "Let's get this over with. You want it to fit, don't you?"

Megan nodded. She tried not to listen as Belinda read out the measurements, making little snide comments as she wrote them down.

"I'm going to lose more weight," Megan assured her.

"I hope so."

Before long, Megan handed Belinda her bank card, and the dress was ordered. "It'll be here by Wednesday," Belinda said as she returned the card.

"What about shoes?"

"You can either try to match the dress or go with black or a neutral. Maybe bronze. That might be nice."

"Should I order them online too?"

Belinda frowned. "Not unless you've tried them on in a store first. Shoes are trickier than dresses." Now she peered at her watch. "It's almost time for Katie to get here. I need to clean up."

"You're going back to campus?"

"No. Katie and I are meeting some friends."

Belinda disappeared into her room, and before long she was picked up by Katie. Arianna and Olivia were immersed in their movie, Mom was working, and Megan found herself missing youth group. She considered going but knew she was so late that it'd practically be ending when she got there. Then she'd have to explain.

※

On Monday, Megan got the distinct feeling that her friends were acting a little chilly toward her. However, she didn't have much time to think about that since it was the official launch of her campaign. She had hoped to have more help from them in putting up posters and flyers and manning her campaign table in the cafeteria. Apparently they had better things to do.

"How's it going?" Chelsea asked as she stopped by the table at the end of the day.

Megan gave her a shiny campaign smile. "Great."

"I've seen your chocolate bars around."

Megan rolled her eyes. "Yes. They're popular. I'm going to have to start rationing them or I'll be out."

"Maybe save them for the end of the campaign." Chelsea picked up a button and examined it. "Have you been able to put much time into the fundraiser?"

"Time? What do you mean?"

"I mean soliciting donations for the auction. I'm working on it, but we need more stuff, Megan."

"I'll do that."

Chelsea nodded, but she seemed troubled.

"Is something wrong?"

"Well . . . I didn't want to say anything . . . but Lishia and Janelle are getting a little put out. If you know what I mean."

"Put out? How so?"

"They're irritated that you didn't help at the soup kitchen. And that you missed youth group. They feel like you're letting them down."

"I'm letting them down?" Megan stood now. "What about them? They promised to help me with my campaign, and yet I was putting up signs by myself. And I've been handing out buttons by myself and—"

"Hey, don't shoot the messenger." Chelsea held up her hands.

"Sorry." Megan glanced at the clock on the wall. "I'm late for practice. We're starting to work on *Fiddler* today." She began gathering up her stuff, tucking it all into the big magenta bag that Belinda had suggested she use. "I've got to go."

Chelsea nodded. "Well, don't forget about the fundraiser, okay? We really need to work together if it's going to be a success."

"I know." Megan smiled. "And it's going to be a success. I just know it."

Then, as she hurried out of the cafeteria, she noticed Lishia and Janelle standing by the soda machine just watching her. The expressions on their faces did not seem very friendly. It was obvious they'd sent Chelsea to do their dirty work. In a way, she couldn't blame them for being concerned. It didn't look right for her to miss youth group or volunteering at the soup kitchen. It was just that she couldn't help it. At least that's what she was telling herself. Anyway, she would have to do damage control later. Right now, she needed to get to practice.

Megan felt a flush of pride as she walked down the breeze-way. Seeing her posters plastered all over the place was a thrill. And so far, she was the only candidate who had bothered to hang posters. But Belinda had said that was typical. "Some people tease the girl who's first with her campaign," Belinda had told her yesterday. "But trust me, it works. That's what I did. That's what the prom queens before me did. Start early and start strong. Keep it going all the way to the end." She had grinned. "And then just let the good times roll."

As Megan hurried toward the auditorium, her stomach was rumbling. She was so hungry she felt tempted to sneak a chocolate bar. Really, what would it hurt? Just one little candy bar? Besides, she would need the energy to make it through rehearsal. But by the time she was in the auditorium, she'd managed to put away three bars. She dumped the evidence in the trash container by the door but frowned to see the "Make It Megan" wrappers crumpled so forlornly. She gave her mouth a swipe and hoped no traces of chocolate would betray her as she hurried down to the stage where others were gathered.

"Golde!" Jack exclaimed. "You made it."

"Yes. Sorry I'm late."

"Congratulations on the prom queen nomination. That's awesome."

"All right, everyone!" Mr. Valotti spoke loudly. "Let's listen up. I'm glad you're all here, and I hope everyone is pleased with their roles in this upcoming musical. Remember, there are no small roles, only small actors." He began to drone on about how everyone was equally important and how he expected them to give 110 percent and how they needed to start rehearsals on time. The usual routine. Not much had changed since the last time Megan had been in a production.

"With no further ado, let's start rehearsing." He clapped his hands. "Scripts in hand. People in their places. Let the fun begin."

But it wasn't as much fun as Megan had hoped. Even with her script right in front of her, she found herself missing her cues and stumbling over her lines as well as her feet. It was as if her brain wasn't functioning properly.

"I'm sorry," she told Mr. Valotti and Jack after she'd blown it for the umpteenth time. "I just feel a little off today."

Mr. Valotti shrugged. "Well, it's the first day. That's to be expected." He grinned. "By the way, good luck on running for prom queen this year." Then his smile seemed to fade a bit. "I just hope you won't let that election take precedence over our production."

She firmly shook her head. "No, of course not."

"Because, while it's a nice honor, it's something that's only for you, Megan. But this musical is for *all* of us." He waved his arm toward the others as he increased the volume of his voice.

"This is a *group* project where every member is vital to the success of the whole. I want you and everyone here to respect that."

She nodded somberly. "I understand."

"Just in case you get distracted with your prom queen election, I have decided to select an understudy for your part." He pointed to Clarisa Wilton now. "Although Clarisa is playing Grandma Tzeitel, I want her to learn the part of Golde too. Is that acceptable to you, Clarisa?"

She nodded eagerly. "No problem!"

He smiled back at Megan, but his eyes were serious. "Just in case."

For some reason she felt that he'd just raised the stakes on her, or perhaps he'd thrown down the gauntlet. She wasn't even sure which metaphor was correct. She did know Clarisa was talented and dedicated and might possibly do a better job as Golde. Megan also knew that she really wanted to be in this musical. But she would have to work hard to do so.

eleven

"Look," Chelsea told Megan on Tuesday afternoon. "I realize you're overextended."

"Overextended?" Megan looked up from where she was stuffing her campaign goodies into the pink bag. "What do you mean?"

"She means you're in over your head," Lishia said.

"Huh?" Megan zipped the bag closed and stared at her friends.

"You've got too much on your plate." Janelle rolled her eyes.

"So I'm completely taking over the fundraiser," Chelsea explained. "You'll still get credit for it, but I just don't want to take the chance that it could fall apart before we pull it off. It's too important to the soup kitchen. They're counting on us."

"But what does that mean?" Megan frowned. "You're kicking me out of the fundraiser?"

"No, we're cutting you some slack," Janelle told her. "You've got your play practice and book club and who knows what else."

"Don't worry, we still expect some help from you," Lishia pointed out. "Just not as much."

"Like what? What can I do?" Megan asked eagerly.

"If you can spare the time, you can work on the soup bowls," Lishia told her. "That's been getting a little overwhelming. The good news is, we've got lots of bowls made. We just need to get them glazed and fired. Want to help?"

"Sure." Megan nodded.

"I'll have some tasks for you on the night of the event," Chelsea said. "For starters, it would be nice if you were the greeter. You can give people name tags."

"And you're on cleanup crew," Janelle said wryly.

"Sure." Megan glanced at the clock. "Whatever. But I gotta run or I'll be late to practice."

"I'm off to work on soup bowls," Lishia said.

"I've got to make some phone calls for more donations," Chelsea told them. "I've got a whole new list of possibilities."

"And I've got to edit my article for the newspaper," Janelle said. "It's all about the soup kitchen and the fundraiser."

"Thanks, you guys—for everything." Megan smiled and waved. "You're the best."

She felt guilty as she hurried toward the auditorium. Despite Chelsea's gracious attitude, she could tell her friends were irked at her. And she supposed they had a right to be. Like Chelsea had said, though, this was an important event. It shouldn't only be up to Megan to carry it out. After all, hadn't it been her idea? That alone was worth something. Or had it been Chelsea's idea? Suddenly Megan wasn't so sure. But it was time to change gears. As she hungrily chomped on an apple that she'd remembered to pack, she tried to transform herself into Golde.

Today she planned to stay focused as she said her lines with Tevye and put forth her best effort as they practiced the songs. She'd stayed up late last night watching *Fiddler on the Roof*, rewinding the old VHS tape again and again to go over her opening lines and the songs she had a part in. Now she felt confident and ready. She just hoped she could keep it up.

"You're doing great today," Clarisa told Megan as they were taking a break. "Much better than yesterday."

"Thanks." Megan peered curiously at her. "But would you be happier if I wasn't?"

Clarisa laughed. "Not at all. I had the lead in the fall play. It was time to let someone else have the limelight."

"Really?" Megan was surprised at her generosity.

"Absolutely. Besides, you have a better singing voice than I do."

"Thanks."

"And this is your last year of high school," Clarisa pointed out. "I still have my senior year to look forward to. Maybe I'll snag the lead in next year's musical."

"I'm sure you will."

"Can I ask you something?"

"Sure." Megan nodded eagerly. She was so relieved to see that Clarisa wasn't threatened by her and that she was so supportive.

"I was surprised you were running for prom queen." She frowned. "That doesn't seem like you. What's up with that?"

Megan felt her cheeks flush slightly, as if she was embarrassed. Or maybe she was just tired from the scene they'd just finished going over. "I . . . uh . . . it's kind of a long story."

"Oh?"

"I thought it would be an interesting challenge."

Clarisa nodded with a skeptical expression. "I guess . . ."

"My sister was prom queen during her senior year. I suppose I thought I should at least give it a shot."

Clarisa still seemed unconvinced.

Now Megan stood taller, remembering Belinda's lectures on posture. "It was time for me to believe in myself," she declared. "To take on new things. Like the election and next week's fundraiser and this musical. I even started a book club."

"That's a lot to take on."

Megan felt a wave of uncertainty now. "I know. And I need to keep my grades up too."

"Well, good luck with all of that. You make my life sound downright boring." Clarisa smiled broadly. "But that works for me."

"Golde," Jack called from the stage. "You're next."

Megan gave Clarisa a weak smile, then she hurried to center stage with script in hand, mentally preparing herself to deliver her next lines. Today she seemed to be more spot-on than Jack, but in the same way he'd been patient with her yesterday, she was patient with him now. Well, in a Golde sort of way.

By the time practice was over, she felt exhausted. Hungry

too. But then she was always hungry. What was new about that?

"You were great today," Jack told her as they walked out of the auditorium together. "Awesome!"

"Thanks."

"And Valotti was impressed too."

"Really?"

"I could see it in his eyes." Jack nodded. "Yesterday he was wondering if he'd made a mistake casting you as Golde. Today, he was totally confident."

"Cool." Megan fished her car keys out of her bag.

"You have a car?"

"Sure." She smiled at him. "Don't you?"

He shook his head. "Nope."

"How do you get home from school?"

"I usually bum a ride." He chuckled. "And sometimes—don't tell anyone—but occasionally I have to take the activities bus. Man, that's a drag."

"Can I give you a lift?" she offered.

"I thought you'd never ask."

As they walked to the parking lot, he told her where he lived, and she explained that the car had been her older sister's. "My mom wanted me to have it during my senior year so I could help with my little sister and be more independent and stuff. It was kind of a trade-off because my mom's so busy with her job." She unlocked the door.

"Nice trade-off."

When they were inside, he examined the plastic gold heart hanging from the mirror. "That's right. Your sister was prom queen last year. I totally forgot about that."

"You forgot?" Megan felt slightly offended.

He chuckled as he tucked his backpack down at his feet. "Well, guys don't usually pay that much attention to that stuff."

"I bet you know who starred in last year's musical," she pointed out.

"That's different."

"I guess."

"I was kinda surprised, Megan. No offense, but you don't really seem like the prom queen type to me."

"Why does everyone keep saying that?" She frowned, but resisting the temptation to check out her image in the mirror, she kept her eyes on the road. Still, was she really that unattractive?

"Maybe it's because they don't get it."

"Don't get what?" She hit the steering wheel with her fist. "Just because I'm not a slender blonde beauty? Does that mean I'm not fit to be prom queen?"

"No, not at all." He held up his hands defensively. "I'm not saying that, Megan. It's just that it seems out of character for you."

"Out of character? How?"

"I don't know. I guess I think of a prom queen as kind of an airhead, and I never thought of you as someone like that. You always seemed to have more substance."

"Really?" She turned to look at him as she stopped for the light. She was surprised to see him studying her carefully.

"Absolutely. You're a down-to-earth kind of girl."

"Well, thanks." She put her gaze back on the traffic light. "I think."

"I mean that as a compliment. I like girls like that."

She glanced at him again. His chocolate brown eyes were fixed on her with a look of true appreciation. Then a horn honked behind her and she realized the light had turned green. "Oops." She put her foot on the accelerator and smiled.

"Anyway, it's just incongruous."

"Incongruous?" She wasn't stupid. She knew what the word meant, but she wasn't exactly sure what he was insinuating.

"You running for prom queen. It doesn't really make sense."

She was tempted to tell him about Pastor Robbie and *Shower of Power*, but that suddenly sounded perfectly ridiculous. Jack would think she was nuts. Instead she gave the explanation she'd given to Clarisa earlier. "I just wanted a challenge," she told him. "Something that would make me work hard and better myself."

"Oh?" He still sounded doubtful. "I guess I can sort of get that."

"Can I make a confession?" She turned to look at him as she stopped for a four-way stop sign.

"Sure." He nodded eagerly.

"I've been having doubts about it too."

"Ah . . . I can understand that."

"What if I've taken on too much?"

He shrugged, and she realized it was her turn to go.

"It all seemed good at first, but it's like there's so much going on. I guess I'm a little overwhelmed."

"It's the next street," he said. "Left."

"I mean, I wanted to do this to have some success. But I could end up failing. At everything."

He laughed. "Oh, I doubt that."

"Seriously," she said as she turned down his street. "I don't even have my dress for the prom yet."

"It's the third house on the right. The white one." He pointed down the street. "Who's taking you to prom anyway?"

She laughed nervously as she pulled in front of the two-story older home. Tulips were blooming along the walk. "That's just one more little detail I haven't figured out."

"You don't even have a date for prom yet?"

She shook her head with embarrassment. "So now you know the truth. I'm in over my head. My dress hasn't arrived. And I don't even have a date. Some prom queen, eh?"

He laughed loudly. "You're a brave woman, Megan Bernard."

"I guess . . . Anyway, I hope I can trust you with all this," she said a bit uneasily. "I don't really want the whole school to know."

"Your secret is safe with me."

She waved goodbye as he got out. As she drove home, she felt slightly hopeful. Unless she was imagining things, Jack seemed to like her. And he seemed surprised to hear she was dateless for prom. Maybe he would think about this and make an offer. Yes, she decided as she pulled into her driveway, that was probably just what he was doing. Perhaps things were looking up. Perhaps she had this more under control than she'd imagined.

As if to confirm this, she was pleasantly surprised to see a FedEx box on the kitchen table—addressed to her. That could mean only one thing, and a day early too! She tossed down her bag and grabbed up the box, happily ripping into it. "My dress!"

"Yeah," Arianna said as she grabbed a soda from the fridge. "I can't wait to see it."

Soon Megan had the box open, and the beautiful satiny gown poured out. The color was a rich, dark pink, just the color of a ripe raspberry. Holding it up to her, Megan ran to the powder room and peered at her image in the mirror.

"Oh, it's perfect," she gushed. "Belinda was right. This color does look good on me."

"It's really pretty with your dark hair," Arianna agreed. "Go try it on!"

"Okay." Megan hurried to her room, stripped off her clothes, and with Arianna sipping on her soda and watching, she pulled the gown over her head. "Help me with the zipper," she said as she adjusted the dress over her bust and hips.

Arianna set her soda down and came over. After fussing and fidgeting with the zipper for a while, she stopped. "I can't."

"Is it broken?"

"It will be if I force it up, Megan. It's too tight."

"I know it's tight," Megan told her. "That was the plan."

"But I can't zip it."

Megan went over to look at herself in the closet mirror. Somehow the dress didn't look as good as it had in the powder room. "I'll hold my stomach in," Megan suggested. "Try it again."

"Okay . . ."

But after several tries, it was clear that the zipper was not going up. "How bad is it?" Megan turned to peer at her backside in the mirror and was stunned to see it was about two inches too small.

"Maybe you can wear one of those things Mom wears,"

Arianna suggested. "You know, they hold you in and make you look slimmer."

Megan turned around to look at the front of the dress again. It really was pretty. The color was perfect. She tried to imagine how it might look if she lost a few more pounds or had the dress let out a bit. It might work.

"I'll go get one for you to try," Arianna offered.

"What?"

"Spanx," Arianna said. "From Mom's room."

Before long, Megan had squeezed into one of her mom's figure-trimming garments and was slipping on the gown again.

"Much closer," Arianna proclaimed. "You lose a couple more pounds and it might actually zip."

"But I can barely breathe," Megan admitted.

Arianna frowned. "Maybe you should send it back."

Megan studied her image in the mirror. With Mom's Spanx and the zipper partially up, the dress as well as her figure looked a lot better. "I'm not sure. I mean, Belinda seemed to know what she was doing. She thought this would work. Maybe I should just stick with it."

"It really is pretty." Arianna got a barrette from Megan's dresser and made a clumsy attempt at an updo. "And with your hair up like this"—she grinned—"wow, you look so glamorous."

"I wonder what kind of jewelry I should wear."

"Something sparkly, I think."

Megan was starting to feel lightheaded now. "Unzip me," she commanded. "I can barely breathe. I think I'm going to pass out."

Arianna hurried to pull down the zipper. "Maybe you should send it back, Megan."

Megan peeled off the dress and the incredibly snug undergarment, then took in a deep breath. "Not yet. I want to give myself one more week to lose the weight. I'll still have plenty of time to send this back and get the next size up."

"Yeah, that makes sense." Arianna picked up her soda and left.

But as Megan pulled on her comfy bathrobe, she wasn't so sure. Even if she did lose the weight, the dress would still be snug, and she didn't want to pass out at prom. Then she caught sight of herself in the mirror. In her pink fuzzy robe, she looked like a chubby bear. Nothing like what she'd looked like in the satin dress. No, whatever it took, she was keeping the dress. And she was wearing it too!

twelve

Dayton still seemed happy to exchange Megan's tutoring assistance for supporting her campaign. He was even wearing her button. Of course, he was also eating her chocolate bars. But it seemed a fair trade. Except that she was running low. *Note to self*, she thought. *Put in another rush order for chocolate bars*. It might be expensive, but it would probably be worth it by the last week when the campaigning would turn hot and heavy.

"Looks like you're running for prom queen alone." Dayton pointed to one of her posters as they came out of the classroom together. "No one else seems to be putting any stuff up."

"Oh, they will," she assured him. "I heard Amanda telling someone that she's got a really slick campaign. It sounded like she's getting some professional help with it. You'd think that'd be against the rules."

"I don't see why. Besides, it's Amanda Jorgenson. Didn't

you know that girl just floats above the rules?" He rolled his eyes.

"Still . . . it seems unfair."

He nodded. "Yeah, but that's life. And just so you know, I'm sure Hallie's got something up her sleeve too. Now there's a girl who likes to break rules."

"Anyway, I'm glad to have a head start." She tapped his campaign button. "And I'm glad you're in my court."

He grinned. "Hey, I like you, Megan. I really hope you win."

"You're not just saying that because I'm helping you in class?"

He shook his head with a sincere expression. "No way. You're a good kid, Megan." He chuckled as he stopped by his locker. "I know Hallie and Amanda well enough to know they don't deserve this. I honestly hope you win. And I'm telling my friends to vote for you."

"Thanks." As she said this, she noticed Hallie watching them from where she was standing next to her locker. It was hard to read Hallie's expression, but unless Megan was mistaken, the girl was jealous. Okay, the irony of someone like Hallie Bennett being jealous of Megan was a bit hard to believe. But as Megan parted ways with Dayton, she felt certain of it. And she liked it.

In fact, as she walked to the cafeteria, she thought if Jack didn't ask her to prom, which she was hoping and praying would happen, maybe Dayton would. She didn't like Dayton nearly as much as Jack, but he would be a good backup plan.

"Are you going to help me glaze bowls after school?" Lishia asked as Megan joined her friends in the lunch line.

"I want to, but I have rehearsal."

"In other words, talk is cheap."

"Huh?"

"You promised to help glaze bowls, but you can't manage to squeeze it into your busy schedule?"

"How about this weekend?" Even as Megan said this, she remembered that the prom committee was meeting on Saturday morning.

"This batch needs to be in the kiln this weekend." Lishia gave her a you-should-know-this look.

"Sorry. But it's not like I can be in two places at one time."

"Guess you should've thought of that sooner," Janelle told her.

"I'm sorry," Megan said again.

Now Lishia gave her a sympathetic look. "I'm sorry too," she told her. "I shouldn't rag on you like that."

Megan just nodded.

"It's just kinda stressful, you know?" Lishia sighed. "So much to get done and so little time." She waved at Chelsea now. "I hope you're grateful for all that Chelsea's doing. She's really putting a lot of energy into your fundraiser. You should see the silent auction list. It's impressive."

"I thought it was everyone's fundraiser," Megan reminded her.

"Except that you'll get all the glory," Janelle said as she picked up a burrito.

"I don't want all the glory," Megan protested. She took a plain green salad and set it on her tray next to her ice water. She'd heard that diet soda could sabotage her diet.

"Let's stop grumping at her," Lishia said to Janelle. "She can't help that she's got too much going on."

"I really am sorry," Megan told them again.

❧

Despite some shameless flirting and obvious hinting, Megan couldn't get Jack to invite her to prom during rehearsal on Wednesday. She could tell he liked her and enjoyed being with her, but he just didn't seem to get it. Or else he got it but just didn't want it. She wasn't sure. As she left rehearsal she felt slightly defeated. And as she walked to her car, she counted how many days she had left to get Jack to ask her. This was Wednesday . . . and suddenly it hit her.

This was Wednesday—and she'd totally spaced book club. Of course, the real reason it hit her was because Brianna was standing in the parking lot. Almost as if she was waiting for Megan. Thankfully, Jack had gotten a ride home with someone else today. Otherwise he would have been forced to witness what was sure to be an embarrassing confrontation.

"If you planned to just blow us off, you could've at least texted or sent a note or something," Brianna said in a grouchy tone.

"I'm so sorry." Megan dramatically put her hand on her forehead. "I completely forgot book club."

"Duh."

"Was everyone there?"

"Everyone but you."

"I'm really, really sorry." Megan unlocked her car, hoping to make a quick getaway before Brianna got really mad.

"Look, you're too busy for us and we know it. You only put the book club together because you thought it would get you more votes for prom queen. But you know what? We're not buying. So you can just take it somewhere else."

"I started book club because I thought it would be fun."

"Yeah, right." Brianna glared at her.

"I did. I happen to like to read. Not all of my friends do."

"Really?"

"Absolutely. I devoured all of the Harry Potter books. And all of Twilight. And Hunger Games. And a bunch of others too."

"Oh . . . ?"

"I want to continue with book club," she claimed. "We just have to change it to a different time."

"What time?"

Megan frowned, trying to think. "I'm not sure. Probably in the evening. Or maybe on the weekend."

"How about Saturday?"

"Well, Saturday's kind of busy . . . I don't know—"

"See, you're not serious. I knew it. You were just using us and—"

"I am too serious. Fine. Saturday it is. But not in the morning."

"Afternoon doesn't work for me." Brianna frowned. "How about Saturday night? Or are you too busy for that too?"

Megan wanted to say no, but knew she couldn't keep stringing Brianna along without looking really lame. "Saturday night, and we can have it at my house. Okay?"

Brianna blinked. "Really? You won't let us down again?"

"I give you my word. I'll provide snacks too." Even as Megan said this, she felt it was too much. Was she making a mistake? But what could she do at this point? Back out and look flaky?

"Okay. I'll tell the others. What time? Like seven?"

"Seven is perfect." Megan made what she hoped looked like a genuine smile. "I can't wait."

Brianna smiled back and then pointed to Megan's campaign button hanging on her sweater. "Got any more of those?"

"Sure." Megan unzipped her bright pink bag. "How many do you want?"

"One for everyone in the book club."

"Really?" Megan fished out the buttons.

"We do like you," Brianna assured her as she pocketed the buttons. "But we don't want you to let us down. Okay?"

"Okay." It wasn't until Megan got into her car that she realized having book group on Saturday night meant she'd miss youth group again. This was troubling on several accounts, but mostly because she felt like now, more than ever, she truly needed it.

Two things became clear by the end of the week. For starters, Dayton seemed to be coming on to her. Oh, she thought it was her imagination at first. And sure, there'd been a time when she would've enjoyed that kind of attention from a jock. But for some reason, it was slightly irritating. As if he'd gone out with every first-string girl in the school and had finally decided to give a second-stringer a try—that is, if she was even second string. At least that was how she imagined he was thinking. To be fair, he might not have had that in his head at all. Perhaps he was simply grateful for her help in class. And maybe he actually did like her.

"Come on, Megan," he pleaded with her as they walked to the cafeteria together. "Just one date."

She laughed. "I'm sorry, Dayton, but your reputation precedes you. I'm really not your kind of girl."

"But I'm changing. I'm tired of those kind of girls."

She laughed louder. "What kind of girls?"

He shrugged. "I dunno. Whatever kind you think I go for. I'm broadening my interests. I gotta think about college next year. It's time to grow up."

She smiled as she patted him on the back. "That's great to hear. I hope it's true."

"So give me a chance then. Go out with me tonight."

Megan wasn't sure if it was her hard-to-get act (which wasn't even an act) or if he really liked her, but she just couldn't see herself with Dayton Moore. Not on a date anyway.

"I know you and your friends are Christians," Dayton told her as they paused inside the cafeteria. "But that doesn't seem like a reason to snub me like this. Aren't Christians supposed to be kind and loving?"

"That's not why I turned you down." She glanced over to where Chelsea and the others were already getting in line.

"Then just give me a chance." He smiled hopefully. "One date. I mean, we have good times together. We get along so good. Why not try a date?"

"Tell you what," she said quickly. "Let me think about it, okay?"

He didn't look too pleased, but he nodded. "Okay. How about if I give you a call after school?"

"Sounds good." She waved, then hurried over to her friends.

"Looks like you and Dayton are getting pretty cozy," Lishia teased. "You sure that's a good idea?"

"He's not so bad," Megan told them. Then she confessed about how he was pressuring her to go out with him tonight.

"You have to be joking." Lishia laughed.

"He's pretty serious." Megan picked up her tray.

Janelle firmly shook her head. "Big mistake. He's been my neighbor for years and the guy is trouble. Trouble with a capital T."

"But what if he's changing?" Now Megan told them about how he was fun in class. How they got along. And finally how he said he wanted to grow up.

"What a line." Janelle rolled her eyes as she set a basket of fries on her tray.

"I don't know," Chelsea said as she filled her soda cup. "Dayton's not so bad. I think if Megan wants to give him a chance, she should."

"Oh, I'm not saying I want to," Megan said quickly. "I just told him I'd think about it. Mostly to get him off my case."

"Well, you don't have a date for prom yet," Lishia reminded her.

"Yes . . . I'm well aware of that." Megan scowled.

"But she's working on Jack," Janelle said. "Remember?"

"I know," Lishia told her. "But she can't wait too long."

"Trust me," Megan assured her. "I look at the calendar every day." She didn't admit that this dateless situation was not only blowing her prom queen schedule but keeping her awake at night as well. Nor had she told them that her dress was too tight. Or that she was so hungry it took all her self-control not to grab a handful of Janelle's fries, or take a bite of Lishia's cheese pizza, or gulp down Chelsea's Sierra Mist. Taking a deep breath, she reminded herself there were some facts a girl needed to keep to herself.

"Well, Jack really seems to like you," Chelsea assured her. "I'll bet he's already making a plan to invite you to prom."

As much as Megan wanted to believe this, the other thing that seemed crystal clear by the end of the week was that she was making absolutely no progress with Jack. Her get-Jack-to-invite-me-to-prom strategy was failing miserably. No matter how much she flirted, hinted, or attempted to act coy, he was not biting. To make matters worse, it seemed that Clarisa was getting just as interested in Jack as Megan was. In fact, while using the restroom during their break at rehearsal, Megan had overheard Clarisa telling her friend Saundra that if Jack didn't ask her to prom, she intended to ask him. Naturally this made Megan even more determined to nail this.

What was really annoying was how it seemed Jack was enjoying the whole thing just a little too much. Almost as if he knew exactly what was going on. But to be fair, Jack was no stranger to flirtatious girls. He was usually surrounded by them. And despite some rumors circulating around school about why he didn't date, Megan was pretty sure he liked girls just fine.

But after rehearsal on Friday, she was feeling fed up. Not only did Jack refuse her offer of a ride home, but he chose to ride with Clarisa and Saundra instead. Trying not to appear ruffled by this, Megan simply smiled and went her way. But as she walked to the parking lot, she was still stewing.

"Hey, Megan."

Megan was surprised to see Zoë standing by the bus stop. "Hey, Zoë." She smiled and went over to chat. "How's it going?"

"Okay." Zoë nodded as she lit up a cigarette. "I managed to lose the loser."

"Good for you." Megan pointed to the bus stop sign. "Riding the bus home?"

"Yeah. I'd ride the activities bus, but that's so lame." She blew out a long, slow puff. "Besides, they don't let you smoke."

"I'd offer you a ride, except that I'm really not supposed to let people smoke in my car either."

Zoë looked surprised. "You should've told me that last time."

"Well, you were kinda upset and all."

"Still, I can respect that." She dropped her cigarette to the pavement and squashed it out with the heel of her boot. "That offer still good?"

"Sure."

As Megan drove Zoë home, Zoë asked how Megan's campaign for prom queen was going. "So far it looks like you're running unopposed."

Megan laughed. "I know. I'm actually pretty surprised that Hallie and Amanda are putting off their campaign like this." She sighed. "Except that they probably don't see me as real competition."

"I honestly don't get why you want to do that. I mean run for *prom queen*." Her voice was full of disgust.

Megan prepared herself for another one of those you're-not-like-that discussions. Perhaps even a lecture. The thanks she got for giving someone a free ride.

"I mean, seriously, it's so provincial."

"Provincial?" Megan knew the meaning of the word, but she was caught off guard.

"You know . . . old-fashioned and socially backwards. I'm sorry, but I think it ranks right down there with things like beauty contests. I would rather die than be involved in something like that."

"Seriously, you'd rather die?" Megan frowned.

"Well, not actually. But it would be so humiliating. I just don't see why you would want that."

"You're pretty judgmental."

"I have my opinions."

Megan considered her response. "You know, the truth is, I used to think that exact same thing. When my older sister ran for prom queen, I teased her mercilessly."

"Your sister ran for prom queen?"

Again, Megan was irritated. Didn't anyone pay attention to these things? "She ran and she won."

"Oh. So it's some kind of twisted family honor thing?"

"No." Megan thought hard. What difference would it make if she told Zoë the truth? Who would Zoë tell? She already thought Megan was ridiculous for doing this. How much more ridiculous would she sound if she told her about Pastor Robbie and the *Shower of Power*? So that's just what she did.

Naturally, Zoë laughed.

"I know, it sounds pretty silly," Megan admitted. "But I needed something to sort of jump-start me. It was like I was stuck in this lackluster life and I couldn't get out."

"I guess I kind of get that."

"I believe God wants the best for me, but I have to cooperate."

"You think the best for you is getting elected prom queen?" The disdain was back in Zoë's voice now.

"I'm not sure. But there are some interesting things that come with it." Megan told her about the fundraiser now. "The soup kitchen is a good cause, but we never would've thought of it if I hadn't decided to do this." She felt a little guilty since her friends were the ones really carrying this now, although she did plan to help with some preparations this weekend and then at the actual event.

"Well, that's cool."

Megan pulled up by Zoë's house. "It's also made me more friendly," she confessed. "It's gotten me out of my shell. Like I'm willing to make a fool of myself . . . sort of. Really, I think lots of good things will come out of it. Even if it is provincial."

"I'm sorry." Zoë gave her an apologetic smile. "I guess I was jumping to conclusions. I'll try to be more open-minded."

"Thanks."

"And thanks for the ride. Beats the bus."

"Hey, Zoë . . ." Megan said before she closed the door. "Would you ever want to go to youth group? I mean, you used to go. There are some pretty cool kids there. And the music is good. Would you—"

"Sure." Zoë nodded. "Why not?"

Megan tried to mask her surprise. "Cool. How about if I pick you up?"

"Okay. I assume it's same time and same place as it's always been?"

Megan nodded, but she could hear her phone ringing. "That might be my little sister," she said. "I better get it."

"See ya!" Zoë closed the door, then waved.

"Hey, Megan." It was Dayton.

"Hey, Dayton. What's up?"

"What's up is that you promised to think about it. Remember?" He sounded hopeful.

She closed her eyes and leaned back in her seat, trying to think of a graceful way to get out of this. "That's right. I almost forgot."

"Anyway, I just checked the movies and there's a new Brad Pitt flick playing, and I had to ask myself, what chick doesn't like Brad Pitt?"

"Oh, yeah . . . I did sort of want to see that." She'd actually read the review and was eager to see it, but she was still unsure. Going out with Dayton?

"So whaddya say? Wanna give it a shot? I promise to be on my best behavior, and if you have a lousy time, you never have to go out with me again. Okay?"

"But will we still be friends?"

He laughed. "I hope so."

She remembered Chelsea's encouragement about Dayton now. And of all her friends, Chelsea seemed to have the most common sense. "Okay. It's a date."

"Cool. How about I pick you up around seven?"

"Sounds good."

As she drove home, she was assaulted with doubts. Really, what was she doing? Everyone knew that Dayton had a reputation for going through girls like Kleenex. Yet they'd been having such a good time being friends. And he was even promising to be on his best behavior. It was possible that she was actually a good influence on him. And perhaps she'd been misjudging him. Maybe it was similar to how Zoë had misjudged Megan earlier. That had felt unfair. And didn't everyone deserve a second chance?

thirteen

As it turned out, the movie was a disappointment, but Dayton, true to his promise so far, had been a gentleman. "I had a good time," she told him as he drove her home.

"Me too."

Now Megan was getting uncomfortable. The whole ending the date by walking to the front door part was worrying her. For some reason she wasn't expecting Dayton to just drop her off in the driveway and take off. Especially after he'd politely opened doors for her all evening. Who knew the guy had such good manners? But if he did walk her to the door, would he expect a goodnight kiss? If so, would she go along with it? If she did go along with it, would that mean that she was really interested in him? And if not, would she be sending him the wrong message?

All these questions tumbled through her mind as he turned

off his engine in front of her house. "Thanks for going out with me, Megan."

"Thanks," she said. "I really did have fun."

"Enough fun to try it again?"

She shrugged, then smiled. "Maybe."

"This whole hard-to-get thing really works, doesn't it?"

"Huh?" She peered at him in the dim light.

He grinned. "You know, keeping me at arm's length and acting uninterested. It really works."

"It's not an act, Dayton. I'm honestly not sure I want to get, uh, really involved. You know?"

He looked disappointed now.

"Just trying to be honest," she confessed.

"Yeah . . . I get that." He hopped out of the car now, hurrying over to her side to open the door for her.

"You have really nice manners," she told him as he walked her to the door. "I like that."

"My dad kinda trained me to be like that. It seems like girls appreciate all that stuff."

She stopped on her front step and stuck out her hand for a handshake. She knew it was a corny gesture, but it was the best she could come up with. He looked surprised, then grasped her hand and pulled her close to him, bending down as if he was going to kiss her on the mouth. But he kissed her forehead instead.

She tried not to look too surprised as he released her.

"See, I can play hard to get too."

She laughed.

"So, tell me, Miss Hard-to-Get, since you're without a boyfriend, who is taking you to prom anyway? I mean, you are running for prom queen, aren't you? Isn't a prom queen supposed to have a king by her side, even if they aren't actually elected like the girls are?"

She frowned. She knew she should be flattered. Lots of girls would be thrilled to have Dayton Moore take them to prom. But this just wasn't how she'd planned it.

"Or maybe you've had other offers?"

"No . . ." She forced a smile. "No other offers."

"Well, I want to go to prom. And I sure don't want to take Hallie, although she's been hinting."

"Why did you guys break up anyway?"

He rolled his eyes. "She's way too clingy."

Megan laughed. "Someone should teach her to play hard to get."

He nodded.

She glanced at the front door. Chances were Arianna was peeking through the peephole right now. "Anyway, it would probably be fun to go to prom with you."

"Yeah," he said eagerly. "We could have a good time. Who knows, you might even be crowned queen."

"Really? You think so?"

"I think you have a good chance. Especially since Hallie and Amanda don't even seem to be campaigning."

"They will."

"I've always kind of thought I'd make a good prom king." He grinned and stood tall. "You know, the kings are actually elected in some schools. I guess we're a little behind the times at Kingston."

She studied him for a moment. No doubt, he was good king material. She probably couldn't do any better. He was already friendly with everyone in school, and thanks to sports, he had lots of fans. It could only be helpful to her campaign if everyone thought she and Dayton were a couple.

"Okay." She stuck out her hand again. "If you really want to take me to prom, I'd like to go with you."

His brows arched. "Cool."

"But . . . if you don't mind . . . I still want to take this relationship slowly, okay?" She peered hopefully up at him. He almost looked amused, like this was some kind of cat and mouse game. Maybe it was.

❧

On Saturday morning, Megan dressed carefully before she went to Starbucks, where the prom committee was meeting. Of course, she felt like a misfit with these girls, and she could tell they felt the same about her. But she tried to fit in. She tried to be helpful. She even mentioned a couple of things that Belinda had told her, trying to sound like she was a prom expert. In the end, she wound up being assigned the cleanup committee.

"We wouldn't need to clean up," Hallie said in a grumpy tone, "if we could afford to rent a ballroom like they used to do."

"We've already been over that," Amanda told her. "The administration has put a ceiling on ticket prices so that all kids will feel welcome at prom. We have to use the gym."

"Which makes decorations seriously challenging," the head of the decorating committee complained.

"I could help with that," Megan offered.

"As well as heading up the cleanup crew?" Amanda's brows arched.

"Well . . . I actually meant instead of cleanup."

"Forget it," Hallie told her. "Cleanup is the only committee we're missing now."

"Sorry." Amanda gave Megan a politely sympathetic smile. "But you did come to the party late, you know."

"I guess it's only fair." Megan forced cheer into her voice for Amanda's sake.

"Every job is important," Amanda assured her.

Hallie laughed. "Yeah . . . and good luck on the restrooms."

"The restrooms?" Megan was shocked. "Won't the school custodians take care of that?"

"Yes," Amanda told her. "Hallie's just jerking your chain."

By the time Megan made it over to Chelsea's to help, as promised, with getting some things ready for next week's benefit, she was feeling worn out. She knew this was due as much to her lack of food as to her busy schedule. She tried to act like she was holding up just fine. She tried to be cheerful and helpful and positive, but it felt like such an act. Finally, when she had to excuse herself while they were still working on posters, her friends questioned her.

"First you come late," Janelle pointed out. "Then you leave early?"

"I'm sorry," she told them again. "I'm hosting book club at my house tonight and I still have to go to the store for some snacks and stuff. I promised the girls."

"Book club tonight?" Lishia questioned. "What about youth group?"

"I know . . . I know . . ." Megan looped the handle of her

bag over her shoulder. "I wasn't thinking too clearly when I agreed to it. But after blowing book club off last week, I felt I owed them this."

"Seems like you're ending up owing a lot of people a lot of things," Janelle said in a snippy tone. "Not to mention your real friends."

Megan tried not to show her irritation over this. After all, a prom queen was gracious. Still, it seemed like Janelle had been on her all afternoon. And even though Lishia and Chelsea seemed happy for Megan for finally securing a date for prom, Janelle had been a wet blanket, acting like Dayton would only be interested in one thing after prom was over.

As Megan wheeled a cart through the grocery store, she tried not to be angry at Janelle. In a way, Janelle was simply expressing Megan's own worst doubts. On the other hand, doubts and naysayers would not earn her the crown. Still, as she loaded a package of chocolate mint cookies into the cart, she wondered if she cared as much about being prom queen as she had a few weeks ago. If she'd known then what a long ordeal it would be, would she still have gone for it? Of course, it was too late to back out now.

Holding her head higher and reminding herself of how a prom queen walks, Megan stopped shuffling her feet down the junk food aisle. Really, she decided as she put a large bottle of soda in the cart, she was on top of her game. Already a solid week into her campaign, she was gaining support and momentum with each day. She had a date for prom who was both popular and attractive. The fundraiser was just days away—and from the looks of things, and thanks to her friends, this event was sure to be a success.

Another success turned out to be her book club that night. Whether it was due to having it at her house or the refreshments or the fact that Megan pretended to have read and enjoyed the book, all the girls seemed to have a really good time. They stayed late.

As they were gathering their stuff to leave, they thanked her and even offered to help her with her campaign. She explained about the fundraiser and how they could still use some extra hands following the dinner and auction. "You know, it's for a really good cause," she assured them. "The soup kitchen downtown will benefit."

The book club agreed to be the cleanup crew. Not only did it get Megan off that particular hook, but she thought her friends would be pleased at her ability to recruit help like that. She waved goodbye and closed the door, letting out an exhausted sigh of relief. That was over.

As she began to clean the living room where they'd met, she commended herself for her good discipline during book club. Carefully avoiding the calorie-laden snacks, she'd simply sipped her Diet Coke and munched celery sticks. She was just about to pour the leftover cookies into the bag when her resolve and self-control completely dissolved. She was so hungry!

Almost unconsciously, she polished off the rest of the cookies. Then she laid into the chips and the Peanut M&M's and everything that remained behind. Feeling foolish and frustrated, she went to bed with a stomachache and very low self-esteem. She promised herself she would do better tomorrow.

Megan felt exhausted after church, as if she'd run a race and could barely put one foot in front of the other. All she wanted to do was to go home and sleep for the rest of the day. But she'd promised Lishia that she'd help glaze bowls today. So instead of looking forward to a long afternoon nap, she was driving Lishia and herself toward school, where the art room would be opened up for several hours so that volunteers could finish the last of the soup bowls. Hopefully a bunch of people would be there, and perhaps Megan could even slip out unnoticed.

"I don't see many cars here," she told Lishia as they parked by the back entrance to the art room. Mrs. Steiner was just unlocking the door.

"Hello, girls," she called as she disarmed the security alarm. "Come on in."

"I guess we're the first ones here," Lishia said as they went inside.

"Or the only ones." Megan set her bag on a table.

"Looks like we've got our work cut out for us today." Mrs. Steiner turned on the lights in the pottery room, revealing stacks of more soup bowls. "I think there are about seventy or so to do."

"Let's attack." Lishia pulled on a paint-splattered shirt. "That's more than twenty each. It usually takes a good five minutes or longer to do one."

Megan frowned up at the clock, doing the math in her head. "That means, with just us, we'll be here a couple hours."

"At least."

As it turned out, they were there nearly three hours, and by the time Megan got home, it was close to five. She still had homework, but all she wanted to do was sleep . . . and eat.

As motivation for continuing on her diet and not giving in to her hunger pangs, she forced herself to try on the prom dress again. She tugged it on but still couldn't get the zipper up. Now prom was less than two weeks off. What if she *never* fit into this dress? Then she remembered Mom's Spanx. Worst case scenario, she'd resort to that. And really, two weeks was long enough to lose five pounds. "Think positively," she told herself as she peeled off the dress.

"Want to eat with us tonight?" Mom called into her room. "I put a frozen lasagna in the oven, and it'll be done around six."

"No thanks," Megan answered as she hung the pretty garment back in the closet.

"Megan?" Mom came into her room as Megan was pulling on sweats.

"Uh-huh?" Megan slumped down into her desk chair and heaved a weary sigh.

"Are you still doing that crazy diet?" Mom peered down at her with a concerned expression.

"It's not a crazy diet."

"It's not a sensible way to eat." Mom frowned.

"I thought you'd be happy that I'm eating vegetables."

"Vegetables are fine. But living on celery, cucumbers, and diet soda is not a balanced diet."

"I eat other things too."

Mom sat on the edge of Megan's bed. "I'm worried you're wearing yourself out, Megan. Working so hard on your campaign and the fundraiser and then this diet. It's not good for you."

"It's only for a couple more weeks. The fundraiser will be done after Wednesday."

"But will you last that long?" Mom's brow creased. "It's like my mother used to tell me—you're burning your candle at both ends. Eventually it'll catch up with you."

Megan picked at the hole on the knee of her sweats and shrugged. "I'm fine, Mom."

"You've never been my high-energy girl, Meggie." Mom leaned forward, peering at her. "I can tell you're exhausted."

"I'll admit I'm a little tired." Megan sighed. "But really, I'm okay."

"What about your schoolwork?"

"What about it?"

"Is it suffering?"

"No, of course not."

"Well . . ." Mom stood slowly. "How about joining us for lasagna. It smells really yummy."

"I know." Megan sniffed the air, wishing her mom hadn't opened her bedroom door to let it waft in.

Mom touched Megan's cheek. "Really, Megan, you don't look healthy to me."

"I'm just tired." Megan nodded to her computer. "And I still have a lot of homework."

"Okay." Mom went to the door, then paused.

"Maybe I'll have some lasagna later." Megan forced a smile. "If there's any leftovers."

Mom laughed. "Of course there'll be leftovers. Good grief, it's big enough to feed eight."

But as Mom left, Megan knew she was going to avoid that lasagna like the plague. To get rid of the tempting smell, she sprayed some cologne in the air and closed her door.

It wasn't until ten o'clock that Megan lost her self-control.

She sneaked into the kitchen and sliced into the lasagna. She didn't even warm it up, just ate it cold with her fingers. Then she got a plate and cut another piece. Once again, she went to bed with a stomachache and a guilty conscience. Who was she fooling anyway? Some diet!

⁂

Megan was barely inside the school on Monday morning when she noticed that Amanda Jorgenson and Hallie Bennett had both begun their campaigns for prom queen. Of course, their signs were bigger and brighter and fresher looking than hers. Not only that, but someone had drawn felt pen mustaches on some of her posters.

"I kind of expected that," Megan told Lishia as she paused to pull down a ruined poster hanging outside the commons.

"It does seem ironic that the graffiti appeared at the same time the other girls' posters went up," Lishia said wryly.

Megan glanced over to where both Amanda and Hallie had set up campaign tables on opposite sides of the commons. Amanda's table was decorated with balloons, and her boyfriend, Tyler, was handing out some kind of goodies to a small crowd.

"Are those cupcakes?" Lishia asked.

"Who cares?" Megan shrugged.

"I didn't have breakfast," Lishia admitted.

Megan glared at her. "You'd go eat the enemy's food?"

"Hey, if I eat one of Amanda's cupcakes, that's one less for her to give away."

"Whatever." Megan was setting up her own table now, arranging her campaign goodies and dwindling supply of chocolate bars.

"I'll be right back," Lishia promised as she headed for Amanda's table.

"What's up?" Dayton asked as he joined her, helping himself to a chocolate bar.

She tried not to show her dismay as he tore off the wrapper and bit into the bar. "Just setting up for business," she said in a forced cheery tone. "How are you doing?"

He grinned with chocolate on his teeth. "Great." Now he picked up a button, and as he was pinning it on his shirt, Lishia returned with both a cupcake and a large heart-shaped sugar cookie.

"Amanda's giving away cookies too?" Megan frowned.

Lishia turned the cookie so Megan could see where Hallie's name was written in pink icing, then took a bite out of it. "Someone's a good cook."

"Not Hallie," Dayton told her. "She made me cookies once and they tasted like dog biscuits."

Lishia laughed. "Well, these are good."

He nodded. "Guess I better go find out for myself."

Megan was tempted to stop him but remembered Lishia's rationale—one less cookie for someone else. Still, it irked her. If her friends acted like they were interested in the other girls' campaigns, it would reflect poorly on her.

"You're not in the hospital after all?"

Megan looked up to see Zoë glaring at her. "Huh?"

"I thought you'd been in a car wreck or something."

"Why?"

"Because you promised to take me to youth group with you on Saturday and never showed."

Megan slapped her forehead. "Oh, Zoë, I'm so sorry. I totally—"

"Never mind. I didn't really want to go anyway." Zoë picked up a chocolate bar and ripped the wrapper off, dropping it on the table.

"But I didn't mean to—"

"Forget it." Zoë rolled her eyes, then turned her back to Megan and walked off.

"What's wrong with her?" Chelsea asked as she joined Megan at the table.

Megan confessed her faux pas.

"Oh, that's too bad. You should've told us, we could've taken her."

"I would've, but I completely forgot. I had book group and—"

"Too much on your plate?"

Megan shrugged. "Maybe."

"Well, in a few days the fundraiser will be behind us. Then maybe we can help you more."

Megan brightened. "That'd be nice."

"Are those *cupcakes*?" Chelsea's eyes lit up.

Megan just nodded. How was she supposed to compete with that?

fourteen

By Wednesday afternoon, Megan felt like she was running a marathon—and she was still not halfway through it. Besides some last minute details regarding the fundraiser that night, Megan had been staying up late trying to learn her lines and songs for *Fiddler on the Roof* and trying to keep up with homework. Plus, this morning she'd met her book group girls for a seven o'clock breakfast meeting.

As she trudged toward the cafeteria to spend some time at her campaign table, she felt more like giving up than ever. How could she possibly keep this up?

"There you are," Lishia said cheerfully as she came up to the table. She set a cardboard box of soup bowls down. "Those are heavy."

"Oh . . . hey." Megan feigned a smile as she peeked at the colorful bowls. "Those turned out good."

"Are you okay?" Lishia peered curiously at her. "You look beat."

Megan just nodded. Lishia had no idea.

"You guys ready to do some decorating?" Janelle entered the cafeteria with two grocery bags in her arms.

"Decorating?" Megan frowned.

"For the fundraiser," Janelle said with irritation. "Remember your special project?"

Now Chelsea was coming toward them with two large buckets filled with fresh flowers. "Check out these blooms," she called. "Le Fleur's donated them to us. They said they're a little old but still good for a one-nighter."

"Pretty."

"I've got a bunch of old canning jars that Kate's loaning me to put them in—you know, for vases," Chelsea explained. "We'll tie those with raffia. Kind of a homespun look."

"Oh . . . nice." Megan nodded.

"Let's get to work," Chelsea said.

Megan knew that meant her too. So instead of "manning" her campaign table, which no one seemed interested in anyway, she made a pretense of helping her friends for a while. Finally she knew she had to make some excuses or risk being late to rehearsal. "I wish I could stay longer," she told Chelsea as she started to pack up the stuff from her campaign table. "This is really fun. But I have play practice."

"Oh . . . ?" Chelsea just nodded, but she was obviously disappointed. "I thought maybe they'd let you have this one afternoon off."

"I don't know . . ." The truth was, Megan hadn't even thought to ask. But it seemed a little late now.

"You're bailing on us?" Janelle demanded as she carried

in another box. "There's a bunch of boxes that still need to be unloaded."

"I have to get to rehearsal," Megan explained.

"Yeah, right." Janelle rolled her eyes. "Too busy."

"I'm sorry."

"We'll be fine," Lishia told Janelle. "I asked a couple guys from art to help bring stuff in. They'll probably be here soon."

"Go ahead and go," Chelsea told her.

"I'm really sorry," Megan called as she grabbed up her bag and took off. But as she was leaving she could hear Janelle still murmuring about how Megan managed to get out of everything. *Do not react*, Megan told herself as she exited. As she hurried to the auditorium, she reminded herself of the goal. *A prom queen has dignity . . . A prom queen is gracious and kind to everyone.* Even if she felt like smacking Janelle, she would control herself.

Of course, she was late for rehearsal. Mr. Valotti seemed short on patience as she rushed up to the stage, where the actors were already in position. "Hope we're not taking you from something important," he said in a tone that warned her not to respond.

"Sorry," she muttered as she dumped her bag in a corner, then took her place next to Jack.

"I guess I'm not needed now," Clarisa said a bit sullenly.

"Thanks," Megan told her. "And sorry."

Clarisa just shrugged, then moved offstage.

Megan wanted to offer a full apology, but Mr. Valotti seemed determined to keep things rolling. After she blew her lines for what seemed the tenth time, though, she could tell he was getting seriously irritated with her.

"Did you go over your lines at all?" he demanded.

"Yes." She nodded. "I thought I had them down."

"Well, you may have to make a decision, Miss Bernard."

"A decision?"

"Which you want more—to be queen of the prom or to be in this musical."

"I want to be in the musical," she assured him.

"Then *be* in it." He clapped his hands, signaling it was time to start a different scene.

Megan's face was flushed with embarrassment as she left the stage. Her heart was pounding hard, and she could tell that tears weren't far off. Plus, she was hungry. She stepped into the shadows, determined to hold it together. A prom queen did not fall apart in public.

"I think he should just let Clarisa take the part," a guy was saying on the other side of the curtain. "All Megan does is mess up."

Megan hurried away to escape that conversation. It was the last thing she needed to hear right now. But in her rush, and thanks to the dim light, she ran smack into Jack.

"Watch it," he said sharply.

"Sorry," she told him. It seemed to be her favorite word today.

"Oh, it's you," he said. "That's okay." Now he looked more closely at her. "Are you upset about something?"

That was all it took—like the dam had broken open, her tears came falling fast. "Come on," Jack said gently. "Let's get you out of here."

Soon they were outside the auditorium, blinking in the bright sunlight, and Jack was looking at her with sympathy.

"I'm falling apart," she told him. "I'm a total mess. I should drop out of the musical and stop running for prom queen and just—just—I don't know. Go live under a rock somewhere."

He hugged her. "No, you shouldn't. You're just having a bad day, that's all." He stroked her hair. "Just take a few deep breaths, and trust me, you'll feel better."

Standing there in his arms, she did take a few deep breaths, and before long, she did feel better.

"See?" Jack released her, pushing a strand of hair away from her face. "So what's the problem?"

Now she began to tell him how overwhelmed she was and how nothing was going as planned. "The fundraiser is tonight, which is why I was late. But I let down my friends. And now I'm letting down the cast and you and . . . I just feel lost."

"Oh, the fundraiser." He nodded. "I forgot that's tonight. Why didn't you just tell Valotti? I'm sure he would've excused you. That's such a great project. Want me to go tell him for you?"

She shrugged. "Just let it go . . . he's busy."

Jack nodded. "Probably right."

"Thanks." She took in another deep breath. "For rescuing me."

"Happy to be at your service. Besides, I was wanting to talk to you . . . alone."

"Really?"

"Yeah. I was thinking about what you told me last week. About the dress and everything and how you don't even have a date for prom."

"Oh . . ." Obviously Jack hadn't heard she was going with Dayton. Why would he have?

"I got to thinking . . . what if we went together?"

"Seriously?"

"Yeah." He grinned.

She frowned. "Is this a pity invite?"

"Not at all. The truth is, I wouldn't have had the confidence to ask you if you hadn't told me those things last week . . . and if you hadn't fallen apart on me just now."

"Really?"

"Absolutely. It makes you seem much more human."

"More human?" She tilted her head to one side. "Versus what? An alien or something?"

"No, versus being perfect. You know, like a prom queen."

"Oh . . ." She thought about Dayton again.

Jack got a worried expression. "Well, now that I've laid it on the line, you're not going to turn me down, are you?"

"No. Of course not." She would have to think of a way to let Dayton down easy. "I would love to go to prom with you, Jack."

"Cool." He let out what sounded like a sigh of relief.

"Wow." She slowly shook her head as realization sunk in. Wasn't this exactly what she'd hoped for? "This is all so unexpected."

"But good, right?"

"Uber-good."

"So . . . do you think we can use your car?"

She laughed. "Of course."

He looked slightly embarrassed as he leaned against the door. "You see, it's kind of hard to ask girls out when you don't even have your own wheels. That's been a big obstacle for me."

"Do you like me or my wheels?" she challenged him.

"Both, actually." He chuckled. "But with or without a car, we're going to prom together. Right?"

"Right." She'd just have to think of a way to make it right with Dayton. Really, why wouldn't he understand? She'd been reluctant to go with him in the first place. It wasn't as if they were actually dating. In fact, the way Hallie had been acting recently, as if she was mad at Megan for stealing her man, which was ridiculous, maybe Dayton would want to consider taking her instead. At least Hallie still appeared to like him. And going to prom should be about going with someone special. Like Jack.

After rehearsal ended, Megan stopped by the cafeteria to see if her friends needed any more help. Other than the kitchen workers, who Janelle had recruited and managed, no one seemed to be around at the moment. However, the cafeteria looked great. Tables were set with colorful placemats and small flower arrangements. The brightly colored bowls were all stacked artistically—probably Lishia's work—on a table by the front door, where someone would collect money. Poster-sized black-and-white photos of people being served at the soup kitchen were positioned on easels, something Chelsea had wanted to do and a nice touch.

Not far from the door, a name tag table was set up, complete with a tablecloth and a large bouquet of flowers. The silent auction items were nicely displayed on some back tables, with signup sheets and pens all ready to use. It was a nice selection of items too, from gift baskets to art pieces to gift certificates. At a glance, it appeared to be worth at least a couple thousand dollars! Impressive. Chelsea had really outdone herself on those. This event was bound to be a huge success.

Most promising, in Megan's starved opinion, was the delicious aroma of food cooking wafting from the kitchen just now. She was tempted to slip back there and check it out firsthand, but, worried that her intense hunger might get the best of her, she decided to go directly home, where she would take a short nap and then dress carefully for tonight's event. She needed to put her best foot forward. Especially since Chelsea had mentioned that someone from the newspaper had promised to stop by for some photos. It would be an excellent publicity opportunity for a prom queen candidate.

fifteen

D on't you need to get to the fundraiser?" Megan opened
her eyes to see Mom staring down at her with a worried look.

"Huh?" Megan sat up.

"It's nearly six. I thought you said you—"

"Yikes!" Megan shot out of bed. "I gotta go." Running
about her room, she grabbed the clothes she'd laid out and
began pulling them on.

"Do you want to ride with Arianna and me since you're
running late anyway?"

"Sure—if you're ready."

"We're ready." Mom frowned at her.

"I'm coming," Megan told her. "Just give me a couple
minutes."

"We'll be in the car."

Megan growled as she pulled a brush through her hair.
This was not how she'd meant this to go. Besides looking

bedraggled, she was already nearly thirty minutes late. The dinner didn't officially begin until six, but the plan had been to be there early . . . to help.

Mom dropped Megan at the front door, and Megan hurried in with a group of people who got in line at the bowl table to purchase tickets from Lishia. At a glance, there appeared to be thirty or forty people already milling about.

"Sorry I'm late," Megan told Chelsea, who was manning the name tag table.

"I tried to call." Chelsea smiled as she handed a couple their name tags.

"My phone is dead."

"Aha." Chelsea gave Megan the permanent marker. "Well, you can take it from here. I need to check on the silent auction. Someone had some questions about one of the certificates."

"Everything looks great," Megan said as Chelsea was turning away. "Awesome."

"This is such a lovely event." An elderly woman told Megan her name for the name tag. "It's refreshing to see young people involved in helping out the community."

"Yes, well, the soup kitchen is a very worthy cause." Megan smiled at her. "Thanks for coming."

As Megan greeted people and made them name tags, she reminded herself of the qualities of a prom queen: kind, friendly, helpful, encouraging, positive. Before long, she felt completely comfortable and was actually enjoying herself. Everyone was so appreciative of the event. So happy to be there. And when it was time for the entertainment, Bethany Bridgewater and her friends in Joyful Sound did not disappoint. They sang and danced with energy and enthusiasm, and the crowd clapped loudly when they finished. However, as they were leaving, Megan noticed that Bethany had an unhappy expression, as if something was wrong. Perhaps she'd figured out that Megan was using this fundraiser for prom queen publicity and didn't approve. Just in case, Megan went over to speak to her. "Is everything okay?" she asked.

"Oh, yeah." Bethany gave her a bright, pretty smile, then leaned over to rub her knee. "I've just been having some leg aches when I dance. My dad says it's growing pains."

Megan grinned in relief. Bethany wasn't upset with her. "Oh, well, you're so petite. It probably wouldn't hurt to grow some."

Bethany wished her good luck with her prom queen campaign and returned to her show choir friends.

As the evening wore on, with everything going so smoothly and everyone seeming to enjoy this event, Megan almost began to believe that she really was the one responsible for the fundraiser's success. Oh, she knew her friends had done most of the work, and for that she was truly thankful. But the idea to run a fundraiser had been hers. Didn't she deserve some credit for that? And it felt good to succeed at something this big—especially after some of the frustrations she'd experienced today.

However, there was one fly in the ointment tonight. Both Jack and Dayton had come to the dinner. Although Megan managed to keep herself busy—or at least appearing to be busy—she had to be congenial to both of them. That felt awkward. Still, she knew the time would come to let Dayton down. Just not tonight.

"This is a great event," Jack told her as he joined her back by the kitchen. "Very cool."

"Thanks." Megan smiled happily. "I have to admit, I'm relieved it's almost over. I mean, it's been fun, but what a lot of work." Of course, she knew it was work she hadn't fully contributed to. And despite the general good feeling of success, she did feel guilty. She also felt that her friends were treating her a bit coolly.

"Okay, everyone," Chelsea was saying from the microphone over by the silent auction items. "Can I have your attention?" The girls had been taking turns making announcements over the PA system, encouraging the guests to bid more, describing various items that seemed to be going for too little, and just generally clowning around. "As you can tell by the clock, the silent auction is about to end. In fact, we have less than five minutes left now, so if you want to make your final bids, you'd better get to it. In the meantime, I'd like to invite Megan Bernard back up here. Some of you may not be aware of it, but Megan is running for prom queen this year. She was the instigator behind this fundraiser. It was her idea." Chelsea held out the mic. "Come on up here, Megan."

Feeling a bit uncomfortable about this unexpected attention, Megan hurried to join Chelsea. They exchanged quick glances, but Chelsea simply smiled and handed her the mic. "Here she is—Megan Bernard, the reason we're all here to help out the soup kitchen tonight."

The room erupted into enthusiastic applause, and suddenly Megan was looking into the happy faces of all the guests. "I want to thank you all for coming tonight," she began. "When we first started planning this thing, we had no idea what we were getting into. But as you can see, it all seemed to work out just fine." More clapping. "Of course, a lot of help went o creating tonight. I certainly couldn't have done it on my own." She rambled on a bit, talking about the soup kitchen and how she and her friends sometimes volunteered down there and how it was great to help others in need.

Finally Chelsea rejoined her, pointing to the clock. "Okay, everyone, put those pens down. The silent auction is officially closed." She nodded to the people who were helping gather the bid sheets. "We'll begin announcing the winners of the prizes in about five minutes, and then you can go to the cashier in back to pay for your purchases." She waved at her dad and stepmom, who were just setting up the cashier table. "My parents volunteered to help with that, and since they both work in the retail industry, I guess they know what they're doing." She chuckled. "While I'm here, I want to give some shout-outs to all the other people who have worked hard to make this fundraiser a success." Chelsea began mentioning everyone who'd helped—from Janelle and Lishia to the cooks and even Megan's book club friends, the cleanup crew.

"Back to you, Megan," she called out as Janelle brought up the bid sheets. "I thought you'd like to announce the winners of the auction items."

Megan liked being in the limelight again. She hammed it up as she read who had won which item. The audience seemed to enjoy it too. Finally, she thanked them all again and told them good night. She turned off the mic and looked up to see Chelsea watching her. She wasn't sure what Chelsea was thinking, but something about her expression didn't look completely happy.

"Is something wrong?" Megan asked her as she went over to join her.

"Not at all." Chelsea made what seemed a stiff smile. "In fact, Kate estimates we've made more than three thousand dollars tonight."

"Wow." Megan nodded. "Very cool."

Chelsea pointed to a woman with a camera now. "I think that's the reporter from the paper. You should go talk to her."

Megan studied Chelsea for a moment. "Maybe you should talk to her."

Chelsea looked surprised. "This is your event, Megan. For prom queen, remember?"

"I know . . . but . . ."

Chelsea nudged her. "Go on. I think she wants to get your photo."

"But we should all—"

However, Chelsea walked away now, going over to where her parents were still working at the cashier table. Megan went by herself to the reporter. Smiling for photos, she answered some questions and then went over to where Mom and Arianna were waiting by the door.

"Do you have a ride home?" Mom asked. "It's getting late. And it is a school night, so I think Arianna should get home."

Megan had originally planned to drive her own car so she could stay late and help with cleanup. But now she needed to figure out a ride, and when she asked around, it seemed that everyone's cars were full or, like Chelsea, they were going home with their parents.

"Just go home with your mom," Chelsea told Megan a little bit sharply. "I'm sure your cleanup crew can handle it without you."

"But I—"

"I need to help my parents." Chelsea cut her off. "See you tomorrow."

Megan sighed then, feeling rejected, and went back to Mom and Arianna. "I guess they don't need my help."

As they exited, Mom patted Megan on the back. "You girls did such a great job organizing all this, Megan. I'm really, really proud of you."

Megan just nodded. She wished she felt proud of herself. The problem was, she just didn't.

⁂

It was unraveling—all of it—and Megan just knew it. She could feel it in her bones as she walked across the school parking lot on Thursday morning. Nothing was going to go right today. Try as she might to follow Pastor Robbie's encouragement to think positively, she knew it was useless.

Not just because she'd woken up with a couple of zits. Or because Lishia hadn't wanted to ride to school with her this morning. Or because she knew she needed to sort out this thing with Dayton and Jack. She knew this was going to be a bad day because she had realized something very important last night.

Feeling discouraged and guilty, not to mention hungry, as she'd gotten ready for bed, Megan had resorted to an old habit. A habit that had been left by the wayside when she'd embarked on the fast-lane pursuit of the prom queen title. Megan had gotten down on her knees and prayed.

Well, it wasn't much of a prayer. That was for sure. She'd

barely begun before she realized that something was very wrong . . . or missing . . . or just plain broken. She suspected it was her. So after muttering a lot of "I'm sorry, God," and even more "Please help me out of the mess I've made," she'd given up and gone to bed—then tossed and turned all night long.

Now as she walked into the school, she could feel a disaster rushing at her—like a freight train. Today was going to be a wreck.

"Hey, great fundraiser last night," Amanda Jorgenson told Megan.

Trying not to look overly shocked, Megan simply thanked her.

Amanda pushed a blonde, silky lock behind an ear and smiled. "Even if we are competing for the crown, I have to admit that was a really nice thing you did, Megan. Kudos to you."

Megan attempted a smile. It was only natural that Amanda should approve of the fundraiser. It was simply Amanda's style to be positive and supportive of a good cause. Everyone knew she was not only pretty and popular but truly a good person too. That was just one more reason she would win the prom queen title this year. Not Megan. Really, the contest might as well be over.

Megan watched as Amanda walked over to join some kids gathered around her campaign table. As usual, they were glad to see her. Why wouldn't they be? Megan glanced nervously around the commons as she set up her campaign table. She didn't see any of her friends around. Probably avoiding her. Why not? She would've avoided herself if it was possible.

"Hey." Dayton came over and gave Megan a hug. "Great evening last night. Nice work."

Megan just nodded.

"Something wrong?" He plucked a chocolate bar from the table.

She shrugged.

"Worn out from last night?" He peeled off the wrapper, tossing her rumpled name onto the table before he took a big bite.

Megan noticed Zoë walking by now. Shuffling her feet with her eyes downward and head hanging down, Zoë seemed to be in as low of spirits as Megan. Perhaps Megan was partly to blame. Just one more way she had failed recently.

"Earth to Megan." Dayton was peering curiously at her. "Are you there?"

"Sorry." She looked back at him. "Did you say something?"

He frowned. "Never mind."

Megan bit her lip, trying to remember what it was she'd planned to say to him. "We need to talk."

His brow creased. "Huh?"

"I can't go to prom with you," she blurted.

"What?" He looked shocked.

"I can't go to prom with you," she repeated like a robot.

"You're dumping me?" He was shocked.

"I'm not dumping you, Dayton. We're not even a couple. Remember?"

"I can't believe you're dumping me. Megan Bernard is dumping Dayton Moore?" He shook his head in disbelief.

"I'm sorry, Dayton. But I told you right from the start that it wasn't a good idea."

"Yeah, but you said you'd go."

"I'm sorry, but I—"

"You're a piece of work," he snapped at her. "You come on to me. You give me your poor little me act. Get me to feel sorry for you and invite—"

"You felt sorry for me?"

He glared at her. "Forget it."

"Are we still friends?" she asked meekly, already knowing the answer.

He just laughed. "Yeah, right!" He pulled the campaign button off his shirt and tossed it to the table. It spun off and noisily clattered to the floor. Megan knew everyone was looking at them now. "Good luck with your campaign, because you'll need it!" He stormed off toward Amanda's table. She was giving away chocolate mini-muffins today.

"What was that about?" Lishia asked as she joined Megan at the table.

"I just told Dayton I can't go to prom with him," she muttered.

"Why?" Lishia looked shocked. "Who are you going to go with now?"

Megan explained that Jack had asked her.

"Oh . . ." Lishia frowned. "I mean, Jack's nice and all. But it seems a little harsh to blow off Dayton like that."

Megan just shrugged.

"Especially if you're still serious about prom queen."

Megan felt a lump in her throat. "Maybe I'm not."

"You're *not*?" Lishia's eyes grew wide. "After all the work we've put into this thing? You're not serious anymore? What is up with you anyway?"

"Remember what happened to you last winter?"

Lishia gave her a dismal look, like this was a topic she didn't want to discuss. "You mean with cheerleading and Riley?"

"Yeah. I know you don't really like talking about it. But maybe this is a little like that."

Lishia gave her a knowing look. "I kinda wondered, but I didn't want to say anything, Megan. Especially after you were so supportive of me when I went through all that. What's up?"

Megan felt the lump in her throat getting bigger and tighter. "I've just done it all wrong."

"Did you lie or break the rules or something?" Lishia asked with genuine concern.

"No . . . not anything exactly like that. It's just that I realized something last night. I haven't been acting like a Christian. I haven't even been praying. It's like I turned my back on God."

Lishia nodded. "Janelle was wondering about that very thing."

"She said that?"

Lishia sighed. "You know Janelle. She calls it like she sees it."

"Well, she was right. It's like I fell for that whole *Shower of Power* crud, like I could think it and have it . . . believe it and receive it . . . but I left God completely out of the equation."

"Not good."

"I know, but what do I do now?" Megan felt tears coming now.

"What do you want to do?"

"I want out of this."

"The campaign?"

Megan nodded. She felt like a drowning victim reaching out for a life preserver. "How do I put the brakes on this?"

Before Lishia could answer—if she even had an answer—a small swarm of girls came over to Megan's table. They were all eating Amanda's muffins, which looked temptingly delicious.

"Just because we were at Amanda's table doesn't mean we're voting for her," Molly Green told Megan in a conspirator's tone. "We were just there for the muffins. We really plan to vote for you."

"That's right," Shanda Bancroft added. "We think it's so cool that you did that fundraiser last night."

"And it's even more cool that you're not part of the snooty club," another girl said. "We really don't want Amanda or Hallie to win. We're telling our friends to vote for you, Megan."

Molly peered curiously at Megan. "Is something wrong? Have you been crying?"

That was all it took to get the tears flowing.

"She's had a bad morning," Lishia explained. "She just told Dayton Moore that she won't go to prom with him."

Molly let out a whoop. "Good for you!"

Suddenly the other girls were giving Megan high fives, slapping her on the back, congratulating her for having good sense, and even hugging her. Megan didn't know how to react, so she simply thanked them. Maybe she'd been wrong about today. Maybe it wasn't going to be all bad after all. Who knew she had so many supporters?

"Hang in there," Lishia told Megan as they packed up the campaign things together. "With the fundraiser behind us, it will get easier. Don't give up on prom queen just yet. Maybe there's more at stake than we know."

Megan nodded, but she wasn't so sure. However, she did know that she had to deal with some things. Not only did she need to get her heart right with God again, but she needed to make things right with her friends too. Even though Lishia was being extra kind, there was still Chelsea . . . and Janelle . . . and poor Zoë . . . and what about Dayton? And that was probably just for starters. As Megan walked to her first class, she knew she had her work cut out for her today.

sixteen

As badly as Megan wanted to make things right with God and everyone, all she could manage was to stumble through her morning classes. By lunchtime, she'd made up her mind about a number of things. To begin with, she was finished with her stupid prom queen diet. Now that she really thought about it, that was probably a big part of her problem right from the get-go. A lack of nourishment had affected her brain. No wonder she was so messed up. Well, that and *Shower of Power*. She had to give Pastor Robbie some credit too. But her situation was about to change. Her mind was made up, and she had an escape plan of sorts. Now if only she could carry it out.

As she hurried to the cafeteria she had just two things in mind: a cheeseburger and fries. After that—and after her brain started to operate normally again—she would sincerely and profusely apologize to her three best friends. She would thank them for their help and support. She would commend all of them for their brilliant work on the fundraiser. Then she would announce that she was giving up her race for the crown. Tada!

"What're you doing?" Lishia demanded when she overheard Megan ordering a cheeseburger basket from the lunch lady.

"Having lunch." Megan frowned.

"What about your diet?" Lishia hissed at her, like this was some state secret that no one should be privy to.

Megan shrugged. "I'm done with it."

Lishia looked confused. "What about your prom dress?"

Megan shrugged again.

Now Lishia looked dismayed. "You're not giving up, are you?"

Megan shrugged for the third time as she placed the cheeseburger basket on her tray, making her way to the soda machine, where she began filling a cup with regular Coke.

Lishia didn't say anything as they joined Chelsea and Janelle at their regular table. Nor did Chelsea and Janelle . . . at first. Then, just as Megan was biting into what smelled like the world's greatest cheeseburger, Janelle pointed at her. "What are you doing with that?"

"Eating." Megan proceeded to take a big bite, slowly chewing, enjoying every fatty, juicy, cheesy, salty bite.

"What about the diet?" Chelsea asked cautiously. "And fitting into your dress?"

Megan wished she'd never confessed to them that her dress was too tight. What had she been thinking? Anyway, that was all water under the bridge now. She took another big bite before she set the burger down and looked at her friends. "I have something I want to say."

They waited expectantly.

"First of all, I want to tell you guys that I'm sorry for acting like such a jerk lately. It's like it all just hit me last night," she confessed. "How selfish and shallow and stupid I've been. This whole prom queen thing"—she picked up a French fry and held it up like evidence—"and this ridiculous diet really messed up my thinking. I want you three to know how truly sorry I am for taking you for granted and treating you the way I did. I haven't done my fair share of anything."

"You've been pretty busy with your campaign. Plus you have the musical and book club," Lishia reminded her. "We knew that."

"Doesn't matter." Megan took another hungry bite and continued talking as she chewed. "I'm ashamed at how hard you guys worked on the fundraiser and how I ended up getting all the credit." She pointed at Chelsea. "I didn't even acknowledge *you* last night. I should've told everyone how much you did to make the whole thing a success. And I didn't." Megan felt that lump growing in her throat again, and despite her hunger, she set the burger down.

"Well, it's a relief that you're figuring it out," Janelle said wryly. "About time."

"Oh, Janelle." Lishia shook her head.

Megan started to cry again. "I'm so sorry, you guys. I hope you'll forgive me. Somehow I'm going to make it up to you."

Chelsea patted Megan's arm. "Come on. It's okay."

"No, it's not okay," Janelle snipped.

"Yes, it is," Lishia defended. "We understand, Megan. You've had a lot of stress."

"No, Janelle is right. It's not okay," Megan wiped her

nose on her napkin. "I plan to write a letter to the school paper explaining just how much work you guys put into the fundraiser and how I hogged all the praise and—"

"Not before the election," Lishia said cautiously.

"I'm dropping out," Megan told them.

"You can't," Lishia protested. She told Chelsea and Janelle about the girls who had gathered around this morning and how excited they were about voting for Megan. "It's like she's an everyday girl," Lishia said. "They can relate to her. And they think it's time for an ordinary girl to be prom queen."

"That actually makes sense," Janelle agreed. "If Megan doesn't run, it means Amanda's going to win. And she's won everything already. Time for a change."

"But I don't want to run." Megan picked up her burger again. "I'm done."

"What about all the work we've invested in you?" Janelle demanded.

"Yeah, we're part of this decision too," Lishia insisted. "You can't just bail on us. We did that fundraiser to help your campaign."

"And to help the soup kitchen," Chelsea added. "But I'm with these guys. I think you need to stick to this. Finish it out. Who knows, you might even win."

"But I don't want to win. I don't even care about it any-more." Megan took another bite. "Can't you get that?"

Janelle scowled darkly at Megan now. "You know what I think this is?"

"What?" Megan asked as she chewed.

"I think this is just you being selfish again. It's like you—"

"*Selfish?*" Megan stared in disbelief. "I'm willing to look like a total fool. I apologized to you guys. I'm going to let the whole school know that—"

"Let me finish," Janelle told her. "You just want out and you don't care that we all worked hard for you. Or that other girls want you to win. Or anything. Except that now you've decided it's too hard." She pointed at the half-consumed burger basket. "You're letting your stomach control your brain."

Megan pushed the basket away from her. "I am not."

"You are." Janelle looked at the others for support. "Did you guys hear her saying she wanted to make it up to us for not helping with the fundraiser?"

They both nodded, and Janelle pointed at Megan. "What if the way you make it up is to run the best campaign you can and beat Amanda and Hallie?"

"But I don't *want* to." Megan couldn't believe it. Here she'd thought this was the end of her troubles, that life might turn back to normal, or something close. Now her friends were demanding she run for prom queen. What was up with that?

"I agree with Janelle," Chelsea said firmly. "In fact, it would probably be good for you to finish this thing, Megan."

Megan pointed at Chelsea now. "Why don't you finish it? You would at least have a real chance. I would campaign for you and—"

"Because I never wanted to run for prom queen and I still don't." Chelsea shook her head. "But you did."

"Not anymore!"

"Fine." Janelle hit the table with her fist. "You wimped out on the fundraiser and now you can wimp out on this too."

"Janelle." Chelsea shook her head.

"You don't have to be mean," Lishia said. "Why don't we give Megan time to reconsider?"

Then, as if Megan wasn't even there, the three of them argued amongst themselves, going round and round—almost like she'd been doing in her head—until they finally decided to give Megan twenty-four hours to figure it out.

"That way you can pray about it," Lishia said as she stood to go.

"And sleep on it," Chelsea added.

"Agreed?" Janelle narrowed her eyes at Megan.

Megan gave her unfinished cheeseburger basket one last look of longing, then slowly nodded. "Okay . . . agreed." She knew it was the least she could do. She just hoped she could do it.

For the rest of the afternoon, Megan was determined to act like a prom queen candidate. To do this, she needed to be mindful of three rules: one, be kind, even when you don't feel like it; two, be outgoing and cheerful, even if you don't like a person; and three, maintain your appearance, even if you could care less what you look like. Unfortunately, she couldn't do too much about the third thing since she'd dressed care-lessly for school. But after lunch she did go to the restroom to brush her hair and put on some lip gloss and mascara, promising herself that tomorrow she would do better.

"Hey," Hallie seemed pleased to see Megan as she came into the restroom. "I hear you're quitting the race."

Megan forced a smile for the sake of the handful of other girls in there. "No, I don't know where you heard that, but it's not true."

"Oh, well, maybe Dayton just assumed you'd drop out after he dumped you this morning."

Megan blinked. "Dayton dumped me?"

Hallie smiled cattily. "Oh, haven't you heard?"

"Well, I, uh—"

"I'm so sorry." Hallie put a hand on Megan's shoulder. "I didn't mean to break bad news to you."

"That's not—"

"You do understand that means he *won't* be taking you to the prom, don't you?" Hallie laughed. "Now that would be embarrassing."

"I know and it's—"

"My, it must be awkward to still be running for prom queen without even having a date."

"I do have a date."

"Well, that was quick." Hallie's eyes narrowed. "You don't waste any time, do you?"

Megan didn't even know how to respond to that.

"No wonder poor Dayton dumped you." Hallie shook her head. "No one likes a two-timer."

"I wasn't—"

"Oh, you don't have to explain to me. I just feel sorry for Dayton. Poor guy. Maybe I'll consider going to prom with him after all." She laughed. "Even if it is a pity date. After all, he's really a nice guy . . . if you give him a chance."

Megan just shook her head as the other girls giggled over this. Then, feeling like she'd tucked her tail between her legs, she slipped out of there. That Hallie was smooth . . . smooth with sharp claws, anyway.

By the end of the day, Megan felt completely drained and wondered how she would possibly keep this up. How had Belinda kept it up? How did Amanda and Hallie? As she plodded toward the auditorium for rehearsal, everything inside of her felt like giving up, and she knew it probably showed in her posture. However, she did not care.

"What's wrong with you?"

Megan forced her gaze up and saw Zoë staring at her. "Oh, hey." She forced a weak smile.

Zoë came closer, peering curiously at her. "You look like you're sick or something."

Megan let out a long sigh. On one hand, she was relieved that Zoë was even speaking to her. On the other hand, she felt guilty for not keeping up the prom queen facade. "You want the truth?"

"Huh?" Zoë's brow creased.

"The truth is, I'm sick and tired of running for prom queen."

Zoë laughed.

"I want to quit, but my friends won't let me." Megan shook her head. "I've also been wanting to explain about last Saturday and not picking you up for youth group," she said quickly. "I just had way too much going on. I still do. But I'm really sorry I forgot. I hope you'll give me another chance."

Zoë made a half smile. "Sure. Why not?"

"Really?"

Zoë nodded. "Just for the record, I think that fundraiser you did for the soup kitchen was pretty cool."

"My friends did most of the work," Megan confessed.

"But it was your idea, right? That's what the newspaper said."

"You read that?"

"Yeah. I read the paper sometimes."

"I know . . . I just meant . . . oh, well."

"Anyway, I decided it's cool you're running for prom queen. And I know a lot of kids feel the same way. Like a regular girl might have a chance, you know?"

"Really?"

Zoë nodded. "I know Amanda puts on the sweet girl act, but believe me, I've seen the other side of her a time or two."

"Seriously?" This surprised Megan. Other than being a little snooty, Amanda had always seemed like one of the nicest girls in her clique.

"Oh, yeah." Zoë's eyes narrowed. "She used to pick on me in PE. She'd start in, but then she'd let her friends take over."

"Really?"

"It was back during sophomore year. She quit as soon as she got nominated for homecoming court—she needed to protect her good girl image. But some of her friends kept it up. Plus Amanda never apologized. And even when she acts nice to me, which she does, I can tell it's just an act." Zoë locked eyes with Megan. "At least you're sincere. Or you seem like it."

"I am sincere," Megan said eagerly. "I consider you a friend, Zoë. And I'm sorry I haven't been a better one to you. I'll try to improve."

"Thanks. Anyway, I hope you don't quit the campaign."

"I won't." Megan stood up straighter. "Thanks for the encouragement. I actually needed it just now."

As they parted ways, Megan held her head a little higher and reminded herself of the characteristics of a prom queen candidate. Maybe she could do this after all. For Zoë's sake, she hoped so.

seventeen

Megan was feeling pretty good by the time she reached the auditorium, although her high spirits sunk considerably when she realized that once again, she was late. Mr. Valotti went through his usual diatribe about being a team player and respecting the others by being on time. Although Megan apologized, she could tell that he and some of the cast were getting fed up.

It didn't help matters that she was stumbling over her lines again. When she'd blown the same scene for the third time and several less than kind remarks were made, she was fed up with them and herself. Still, she knew she needed to handle this graciously. She waited until break time and then approached Mr. Valotti. "Can we speak in private?" she asked quietly.

He nodded, leading her down to the seats in the auditorium.

"I think I should do everyone a big favor and just quit

the musical," she told him. "It's obvious that I'm bringing everyone down."

"You do seem to have some torn allegiances," he said solemnly.

She nodded. "I'm overcommitted. And I know it."

"Well, I respect your willingness to admit this."

Suddenly she felt torn. A part of her wanted to be in the musical more than she wanted to run for prom queen. In fact, she realized, it was no contest. Yet how could she be that selfish to the cast? "I would so love to be in *Fiddler*," she said weakly, "but I know it's not fair to the others." She blinked back tears. "So I'll quit. Clarisa can have my role."

He reached out and firmly shook her hand. "Thank you for making this decision, Megan, before we got any further along."

"Thanks for understanding," she said in a gruff voice. No one else was around to see her just now, and more than anything, she did not want to break down and start blubbering in front of all of them. She knew she should find Jack and explain to him. But how could she do it without tears? She would have to call and apologize later. Right now, she just wanted to get out of there.

Megan cried all the way to her car. But once she was inside, she rolled down the windows to cool it off and then called Jack's cell phone and, knowing he'd still have it turned off for practice, she left a message.

"I know I should've told you face-to-face," she explained, "and you've probably heard the news by now. But I quit the play. It was just too much. I realized I needed to focus on my campaign. I was spreading myself too thin." Then she closed her phone and drove home, trying not to cry.

As soon as she pulled into the driveway, she noticed a box on the front steps. Upon closer inspection, she saw that it was her second order of chocolate bars—baking in the sun. She grabbed the box up, taking it into the house, where she tore it open only to discover that the bars were melted. Worried that the candy was ruined, she carefully removed them, one at a time, and placed them in the fridge and freezer. Really, what more could go wrong today?

She went to her room and fell onto her bed, exhausted. All she wanted to do was sleep . . . and hopefully when she woke up, life would look better. However, when she woke, it was to the jarring sound of her cell phone ringing. It was Jack.

"Hey, Jack." She sat up sleepily.

"Did I disturb you?" His tone was sharper than normal.

"No . . . I was just asleep." She tried to focus.

"Well, thanks for letting me know." He was obviously mad at her.

"So you got my message."

"Yeah. Well, first I heard it from Valotti, along with the rest of the cast. That was pretty special."

"I'm sorry, I would've—"

"Do you know what a slap in the face that was?"

"A slap in the face?"

There was a long pause, and she wondered if he'd hung up, but then he spoke. "We auditioned together, Megan. It was kind of a mutual commitment to do *Fiddler* together. At least I thought it was."

"I know, but I was failing at it."

"You could've tried harder."

"I *did* try harder. I just didn't have what it took, Jack."

"You did too. When you were good, you were great."

"But I didn't have the energy. You could see that."

"You mean because of your *prom queen* campaign." He sounded disgusted.

"Yes . . . that and other things. The fundraiser and book club and my studies and . . ." She knew she sounded lame.

"Right." His voice was flat. "FYI, the fundraiser is history now."

"I know . . ."

"So basically you just wanted to quit so you could focus on your prom queen crown."

Megan didn't know how to respond. What he'd said was partly true, but it wasn't really how she felt. Although at the moment she wasn't even sure how she felt. Well, besides confused.

"Anyway, I get it, Megan. You don't really care about me or the musical."

"I do too."

"No, you don't. Not as much as you care about that stupid prom."

"That's not true!"

"So I think you and I should call it quits too."

"You don't want to go to the prom with me now?" Her voice cracked slightly. "You're backing out on me?"

"No more than you backed out on me."

"But I—"

"Anyway, I heard that Dayton was taking you," he said in a hurt tone. "I didn't really believe it at first, but I noticed you two together at the fundraiser, and I suspect that even if he hasn't asked you yet, he'd probably be willing."

"Right . . ." She felt like she was falling into a hole—a deep, dark hole.

"I guess there's not much more to say."

"Except that I'm sorry," she said quietly. "I really am, Jack. I never meant to hurt you."

"Hey, I'm just fine." The sarcasm seeped from his voice. "And Clarisa is thrilled about getting to play Golde. In fact, I might even take her to the prom now."

"Great." She attempted to sound cheerful. "I'm happy for both of you."

After she hung up, she felt sick to her stomach and not even hungry. It was like her life was on a crash course and from here on out, nothing was ever going to go right in regard to this stupid prom. Why should she even try?

She knew it was time to pray—actually, it was way past time. Yet she'd had this gnawing feeling that God might not want to listen to her anymore. Not after she'd been so shallow and selfish and stupid. Not to mention hypocritical, trying to keep up a Christian persona when she'd been anything but underneath. Why should God listen to her? She didn't even want to listen to herself. Still, she knew the right thing was to go to God. But why was it so hard?

Pacing back and forth in her room, she thought about all the selfish choices she'd made these last several weeks. How she'd completely left God out of her life. How she'd fallen for Pastor Robbie's promising words. How stupid could she have been? Just thinking about all this made her feel more tired than ever. If only she could go back to bed and just sleep until prom was over and done with. Then she would reemerge and attempt to put her life back together. If that was even possible. She didn't even want to think about her grades right now. She knew they had suffered.

Megan glanced uncomfortably at the Bible on her dresser. Thanks to her killer schedule and missing youth group, it had gone untouched for the past several weeks. She picked it up now, absently letting it fall open in her hands and wishing she could find some answers there. She flipped to where she'd left a bookmark long ago. It was in the New Testament section, and for some reason her eyes stopped in the middle of a page and she began to read. Blinking at how comforting the words were, she reread the three simple sentences again, slowly and out loud this time. She knew they were words Jesus had said. Obviously they were spoken long ago, but for some reason they seemed to be written just for her.

Come to me, all of you who are tired and have heavy loads, and I will give you rest. Accept my teachings and learn from me, because I am gentle and humble in spirit, and you will find rest for your lives. The burden that I ask you to accept is easy; the load I give you to carry is light. (Matt. 11:28–30)

With these words reverberating through her tired mind, she got down on her knees and began to pray. "Here I am," she said quietly. "You said to come to you. I'm coming. I am tired and I have been carrying a heavy load. Too heavy for me. Please, give me rest." She looked at the next line. "I do want to accept your teaching. I want to learn from you. I want to be gentle and humble like you. I want your rest. Please, help me to find it."

She waited there for a few minutes, just thinking on these things. She began to cry again. But these weren't the desperate tears of frustration that she'd been shedding off and on all day. These were tears of relief and genuine regret. She told God everything she was sorry for—and the list was long—and she asked him to forgive her and to lead her. "If I'm going to run for prom queen, I want to do it your way," she said. "Please, show me how."

When she got up, she felt surprisingly refreshed. It really did seem that a load had been lifted. She washed her face, went into the kitchen, and for the first time in weeks, poured herself a bowl of cereal and began to eat it.

"What are you doing?" Arianna asked as she came into the house.

"Eating." Megan smiled.

Arianna frowned. "But what about fitting into your dress?"

Megan shrugged. "I guess I'll have to get a different one."

Arianna opened the fridge, then held up a chocolate bar. "What's up with this?"

Megan explained about the meltdown.

"Oh." Arianna shook her head. "Bummer."

"You can have one if you want."

"Seriously?" Arianna looked shocked, because Megan had gotten on her for sneaking one last week.

"Sure." Megan smiled. "You know, I never really thanked you for all the help you and Olivia have been."

"You got us pizza," Arianna reminded her as she peeled off the paper.

"Yeah, but I was usually grumpy about it."

"That's just because you were hungry."

Megan laughed. "Well, that was part of it. But I was also doing everything all wrong."

"How so?" Arianna sat across from Megan at the breakfast bar, and Megan proceeded to tell her younger sister about her God moment today.

Arianna nodded like she got this. "That's cool, Megan. Thanks for telling me."

"So I'm going to run my campaign God's way."

"How do you know what that is?"

Megan frowned. "I'm not sure exactly. In some ways it probably won't look that much different . . . on the outside anyway. But on the inside, well, I don't think I'll be nearly so stressed."

Already Megan felt like the stress was melting away from her. Just sitting there peaceably with her little sister, and later on eating Chinese takeout with Arianna and Mom, not freaking over the calories . . . it felt like old times. It felt good. And the food was delicious!

After dinner, Megan went to her room to work on homework and to write two letters. One to Jack and one to Dayton. Both an apology. She tried to keep it short and sincere. Although she knew they might just laugh at her or even read her letters aloud to friends, she was determined to give them to the guys. To sweeten them up and to prevent the guys from just wadding them up and tossing them, she rubber banded each note to a couple of chocolate bars.

Then she went and looked at the dress hanging in her closet. It was so pretty, yet she knew it was never going to fit. Just to be sure, she tried it on once more. There was no way that zipper was going up. Even with the aid of Spanx, if she could get it up, she realized that it would've been extremely uncomfortable. She doubted she would've even been able to sit down in it. And with her luck, she probably would've ended up splitting a seam at the dance. She laughed as she hung it back up. One disaster avoided.

However, when she considered the money she'd wasted on that dress, as well as so many other prom related things, she felt depressed and weary. How could she have been such an idiot? So she got out the Bible and read those three verses again. She gave all her worries about money to God too. It was a burden she didn't want to carry on her own anymore. She also asked God to help her to find a dress to wear to prom—even if it wasn't much.

"It would be nice to have someone to go with too," she prayed finally. "But I probably deserve to go by myself. That would sure humble me." As she said amen, she realized she didn't even care if she went alone or not. It was like none of it really mattered anymore. It was in God's hands now, and that was a huge relief.

❧

Megan felt truly happy as she walked into school on Friday. Without saying anything, she handed off her apology letters to the guys. They looked surprised, but at least—perhaps due to the chocolate bars—they didn't toss them.

She cheerfully said hi to both Amanda and Hallie as she went to her campaign table. And she freely gave away the chocolate bars to everyone and anyone who wanted them, even though she knew they didn't intend to vote for her. It just didn't matter.

"You seem different," Lishia said as Megan was packing things up.

"I am different," Megan told her. "I'll explain it to you guys at lunch."

For the first time in weeks, Megan felt able to focus on her classes. She knew it was partly because she was no longer starving but also because she wasn't distracted by trying to act like Miss Congeniality. Not that she was rude to anyone. She was just more herself. Relaxed and friendly, but not obsessed with earning people's favor—and votes. She no longer cared.

At lunch, she waited for her friends to be present, then told them about her complete turnaround.

"That's great," Janelle told her.

"Very cool," Chelsea added.

"And you're still running for prom queen?" Lishia looked worried.

Megan nodded. "But it's in God's hands. I'm just going to be myself from here on out."

"Good idea." Chelsea nodded.

"Except there are a couple of snags," Megan admitted. "But I'm trusting God to deal with them."

"What kind of snags?" Lishia asked with concern.

Megan explained about being dateless.

"First you have two dates and now you have none?" Janelle frowned.

"That's not all," Megan told her. "Since I dumped the diet, my dress is never going to fit." She giggled. "No dress. No date. No big deal."

Her friends looked shocked.

"Well, it's not too late to find a dress," Lishia said.

"Except that I'm on an extreme budget now." Megan sighed. "I can't believe how much money I wasted on this campaign. If I find a dress, it's going to have to be cheap."

"There must be some bargains out there," Chelsea assured her. "I'll see if Kate's got any ideas."

"And I'm sure we can dig up *someone* to be your date." Janelle tossed Megan a sly grin. "There's always Howard Brinks."

Megan tried not to grimace. Howard was not only the geekiest guy at youth group but pretty obnoxious too. His idea of a good time was pulling "practical jokes" on the unsuspecting. Still, she reminded herself, Howard was a person with feelings, and he was a senior. What if he wanted to go to prom?

"I suppose I could do that," she said quietly.

Naturally, all her friends laughed.

"Wouldn't that be priceless," Janelle teased. "Howard Brinks as prom king."

"Hey, it might be enough to win you the election," Lishia pointed out.

"But not much fun for Megan." Chelsea said sympathetically.

"Well, beggars can't be choosers." Megan shrugged. "Poor Howard might really want to go to prom. Who else would go with him?"

Janelle slapped her on the back. "You really have changed, Megan."

"Well, don't you go asking Howard just yet," Lishia warned Megan.

The girls kicked around a few other prom escort possibilities, but by the time the lunch break ended, Megan knew that they hadn't made any actual progress in the date department.

"Does anyone want to help me go dress shopping?" Megan asked hopefully as she picked up her tray. "I thought I might go looking tonight."

They all had plans, but instead of taking offense that they were too busy for her (like she probably would've done a few days ago), she shook it off. After all, what goes around comes around, and she was well aware of how many times she had been too busy for them. Maybe Mom and Arianna would want to go dress shopping with her.

eighteen

As it turned out, Mom had dinner plans with a business associate, and Arianna was going to a sleepover. But instead of throwing herself a pity party, after they left, Megan put a frozen pizza in the oven and started surfing fashion websites, hoping to get some kind of inspiration for her prom dress.

She was just biting into her third piece of pizza when Belinda burst into the house. "Hey, people," she called. "Surprise! I'm home."

Megan looked up with a string of cheese hanging from her mouth and smiled. "Hey, Belinda, what're you doing here?"

"Laundry." She tossed a big bag into the laundry room off the kitchen, then frowned. "The question is—what are you doing?"

Megan shrugged and set down the pizza. "Having dinner and—"

"Dinner?" Belinda picked up a piece of pizza, shook her

head, then dropped it back down onto the pan as if it were poisoned. "*Triple* cheese? Please!"

"Mom and Arianna are out for the night," Megan said, as if that explained everything.

"What happened to your diet?"

"I'm obviously not on it now."

"But why?" Belinda peered closely at her. "What about prom?"

"What about it?"

"Did you quit the race?"

Megan shook her head as she picked up her slice of pizza again.

"Then what are you doing?" Belinda actually slapped her hand now.

"What are—"

"You're self-sabotaging." Belinda dropped the half-eaten piece of pizza onto the rest of the pizza, then picked the whole thing up, dumped it into the trash compactor, and turned it on.

"What?" Megan growled along with the compactor.

"Come on, Megan. You'll thank me tomorrow."

"You don't understand. I've changed my—"

"I do understand." Belinda folded her arms across her front like an army sergeant. "I talked to Arianna this afternoon. She told me you can't fit into your prom dress."

Megan waved her hand. "So?"

"So?" Belinda looked honestly shocked.

"I'm going to get another one."

"Another one? That one was perfect."

"Perfect on the hanger. Not so perfect on me."

"But you were going to—"

"Look, Belinda." Megan stood, looking directly into her beautiful sister's face. "Short of surgery, I was never going to fit into that dress. Okay?"

"Okay." Belinda rolled her eyes. "I get that."

"I can't run my life or my campaign how you want me to. Like it or not, I just naturally have more, uh, curves than you do. And I plan to find a dress that fits my curves."

Belinda laughed. "How about a gunnysack?"

"Thanks!" Megan turned away.

"Hey, I'm sorry, Meggie." Belinda put a hand on her shoulder. "That was a little harsh."

Megan just nodded. She didn't want to give way to tears.

"Tell you what. As soon as I get a bite to eat, we'll go dress shopping together. Okay?"

Megan brightened as she turned around. "Really?"

"Sure. It'll be fun."

"Great!"

"You go change into something that's easy for trying on dresses while I heat up some low-fat soup."

As Megan went to her room, she had to wonder: Where did Belinda get such amazing discipline? How was she able to toss yummy cheese pizza in the trash and then eat canned soup? It was like she was on a perpetual diet of sorts. Where was the fun in that?

As Megan drove them to the mall with the best formal stores, she questioned Belinda. "Are you always on a diet?"

"Huh?" Belinda put her iPhone down.

"I mean, are you always watching your weight? It's like

you never eat anything that's fattening or sweet or anything."

Belinda laughed. "Yeah." She patted her thin midsection. "It works, doesn't it?"

"I guess." Megan frowned. "But I read that girls who diet all the time can really mess up their metabolisms. You know, when they get older."

"Oh, that's ridiculous."

"No. Someone did a study on it. Women who constantly dieted in their teens and early twenties tended to put on more weight later in life."

"Oh, well . . . that's later in life."

"Don't you care?"

Belinda laughed. "All I really care about is looking my best right now. Why shouldn't I?"

"I don't know." Megan tried to wrap her head around this. "I just hope you're not hurting your health."

Belinda laughed even louder. "Don't worry about me, Megan. You're the one who got caught snarfing down greasy pizza tonight. You should think about your own health."

Megan nodded. "Yeah . . . I guess so."

"And you should be thinking about what kind of dress we're looking for. Lock it into your head so we don't get distracted looking at the wrong ones. There is a science to good shopping." She then began to describe the elements they would be searching for.

"What if the dresses are too picked over?" Megan asked as they went inside the first store.

"I'm sure they are picked over," Belinda said.

"Remember I'm on a tight budget," Megan said suddenly. "I've already spent way too much on this campaign."

"Well, it's not like you can scrimp on your dress, Megan. The dress is everything."

"There's no chance I'm going to win," Megan explained. "I'm just going through the paces to make my friends happy."

"Well, there's no way my little sister is going to show up at prom looking lame," Belinda told her. "Let's get that clear."

Megan resisted the urge to laugh. She hadn't even told Belinda the worst part of all this yet—that she had no date. Still, she just didn't think she could handle the ridicule that would come with that confession.

Maybe it was a night for humiliation, though, because it seemed that every dress Belinda was absolutely certain was one, perfect; two, a good deal; and three, going to fit . . . turned out to be all wrong.

"You never should've given up on that diet," Belinda said as she struggled to zip the back of a hot pink number.

"I felt like I was dying."

"How do you feel now?" She gave a hard tug.

Megan gasped.

"It's not going to fit."

"Duh." Megan started peeling it off. "I told you that already."

"I just figured if we could zip it, we might be able to send it to alterations to get the seams let out."

"Let's just pick one that fits to start with." Megan pulled out a dress she'd selected earlier. It was kind of a plummy pink color, and although it wasn't as stunning as the one in her closet at home, it seemed nice enough. More importantly, it fit—she could actually sit down in it. "How about this one?"

"That looked like a gunnysack on you."

"But it was comfortable." Megan fingered the stretchy fabric.

"Do you need any help in here?" the salesgirl asked.

"Not unless you have some tougher-than-steel undergarments that will trim around twenty pounds from my sister's body."

"We do have some new shapewear—"

"That's okay," Megan said sharply. "All I really want is a dress that fits to start with."

Belinda scowled.

"I think we've tried every possibility here." Megan pushed the dress onto its hanger. "Thanks!" She glared at Belinda now.

"That's it? You're just going to give up?"

Megan felt close to tears now. This was not how she'd wanted this to go, but it was like Belinda was determined to make her feel fat and ugly and like a loser. "You know what, Belinda?" she said suddenly. "I'm not you."

"I know that."

"You've always been pretty and popular." Megan pulled on her jeans. "You were meant to be prom queen."

Belinda smiled slightly.

"I was never meant for that stuff. I've figured that out. I wish I could drop out of the campaign, but my friends have worked so hard, and there are girls who want me to keep running, so I promised to see it through. But just for the record, I have to do it my way." She pulled on her T-shirt, then looked at herself in the mirror. In clothing that fit, she didn't look half bad. She fluffed her hair back into place with her fingers. "And even though I'm not you, I happen to like myself. In fact, I started to like myself a lot more when I realized how stupid I'd been to run for prom queen." Megan actually told Belinda about how she'd turned the whole thing over to God. She smiled as she reached for her bag. "That really takes the pressure off. Because I no longer care about the outcome."

"Well . . . if that works for you." Belinda opened the changing room door.

"It does work for me. It's helped me to focus on the stuff that really matters," she confessed as they walked toward the front of the store. "Like my real friends. And my grades. And looking forward to college next year. I mean, it's just a matter of time until this is all just a silly memory anyway. In fact, it's a memory I'd just as soon forget."

"Maybe it's like that for you . . ." Belinda looked unconvinced as they walked through the store.

Megan stopped walking and put her hand on Belinda's arm, looking straight into her sister's eyes. "Honestly, Belinda, can you tell me that having been prom queen in high school makes your college experience any better? Or makes your life any better? I mean, seriously?"

To Megan's surprise, Belinda started to cry.

"What's the matter?" Megan held on to Belinda's arm, guiding her outside of the store and into the parking lot. "Did I say something wrong?"

Belinda continued to cry, wiping her tears with her hands as they got into the car.

"What did I say?" Megan dug in the console for a fast-food

napkin, then handed it to Belinda. "I'm sorry, Belinda. I think I just got tired of getting tweaked for my weight. Did I say—"

"No." Belinda wiped her eyes. "It's just that it's true."

"What's true?"

She blew her nose and took in a deep breath. "Being prom queen is one of my happiest memories."

"I know." Megan nodded, trying to grasp what was happening. "I didn't mean to suggest it wasn't."

"But you're right—it hasn't helped me with college. Not one bit."

"Huh?"

Belinda sighed. "I'm flunking out, Megan."

Megan blinked. "Seriously?"

She nodded.

"Oh . . . wow . . . I'm sorry."

"I haven't told Mom yet."

Megan knew exactly how much Belinda's tuition and housing cost, and she knew Belinda hadn't secured any scholarship money during high school. Belinda had never worked summer jobs like Megan either. Of course, Megan knew that her silly pursuit of prom queen had depleted her savings a bit, but at least she still had some, and she had scholarships lined up too. That is, if she managed to salvage her grades after the past several weeks, and she was seriously working on it.

"What are you going to do?" Megan asked quietly.

"Quit." Belinda sighed. "Even if I aced my finals, which isn't even possible, I'd barely make passing grades. And combined with all the other cruddy grades, well, the truth is, this whole year's been a total wash."

Megan sighed. So much for Mom's self-sufficiency plan. After the divorce, she'd told the girls that their grades were their responsibility from there on out. She'd read a book that said kids needed to own their academic successes and failures and be accountable for them. Not the parents. Still, Megan knew that Mom would be furious about this. Really, why shouldn't she be? What a waste. Even so, Megan knew that Belinda was hurting . . . and ashamed.

"I'm sorry," Megan quietly told her sister. "I'm sure it must be really hard to admit this."

Belinda just blew her nose again.

"I'm sure you'll figure something else out, Belinda. You're so good at things like fashion and hair and makeup. Maybe there's some kind of career for you in that."

Belinda barely nodded. "Maybe . . ."

Megan wondered what kinds of careers other ex–prom queens usually pursued. Not that all prom queens were like Belinda. Megan knew that Amanda was fairly strong academically.

Belinda sat up straighter now. "I can't believe I told you that," she said a little sheepishly. "You won't tell Mom, will you?"

"I think that's your job."

"Yeah, I know. I guess I'm putting it off as long as possible."

Megan couldn't blame her for that.

"It's pretty humiliating."

Now Megan suspected that might even have been the reason Belinda had been so brutal to her over her weight and the prom queen campaign. That made it easier to forgive her. "Thanks for telling me that," she told Belinda as she started the car.

"So now you can gloat over me," Belinda said sadly.

"I don't want to gloat." Megan waited to put the car into gear.

"Well, I was acting like I was so together . . . putting you down." Belinda shook her head. "The truth is, I'm a total mess."

Megan chuckled. "Well, I'm a mess too. I mean, how many girls running for prom queen still don't have a dress just one week from the big day?"

"You'll find a dress."

"Well . . . there's another thing," Megan admitted as she put the car into drive.

"What's that?" Belinda sounded only mildly interested.

"I don't have a date either."

"*What?*" Belinda turned and stared at Megan. "You gotta be kidding!"

"Nope." Without going into more detail, Megan just shook her head, but as she drove away from the mall, Belinda burst out into laughter.

"I can't believe you're running for prom queen with no date and no dress."

Well, at least Megan had cheered her sister up. That was something.

nineteen

The next day, Belinda attempted to be helpful in locating the perfect prom dress. She even made Megan try on all the old dresses, thinking there might be a way to save some money by transforming one of them into something worthwhile. No chance.

"Well, at least you might be able to use a pair of my shoes," Belinda said as she opened her bedroom closet for Megan to peruse that afternoon. "After all, our feet are the same size." She pulled a black pair of high-heeled sandals out. Strappy with glittering rhinestones on the buckle, they were actually quite pretty. "These go with just about anything that's not pastel."

Megan thanked her. "I'll keep them in mind after I figure out my dress."

"You're sure you don't want to go dress shopping again tonight?"

Megan reminded her she had youth group.

"But this is important," Belinda insisted.

"Youth group's important too," Megan told her.

"But I have to go back to school in the morning. It's my last chance to help you before prom."

"I promised to give a friend a ride tonight." Megan almost pointed out the futility of Belinda returning to college if she was really dropping out. But she knew it wasn't her business.

To Megan's relief, no one at youth group—well, except for Janelle, and that was just Janelle—mentioned her recent absence. They welcomed Zoë just as casually as if she were a regular too. Megan could tell Zoë appreciated it.

When it was time for prayer and share, Megan knew she had to speak out. It would be one more form of humiliation, but she felt it was something she needed to do. So she raised her hand. Then, feeling Zoë's curious eyes on her, she stood and cleared her throat. "I have an embarrassing confession to make to everyone," she began slowly. "Some of you might remember how I made this spiritual-sounding announcement several weeks ago . . . about believing God told me to run for prom queen." She waited, watching as many of them nodded.

"Anyway . . . I have to admit that I was all wet about that. God wasn't the one who told me to run for prom queen. It was my own silly pride. As it turned out, I made a real mess of it. And I wasn't a very good friend." She explained about how Chelsea, Lishia, and Janelle had handled the fundraiser, giving her the credit, as well as a number of other things. Then she told them about her aha moment with God and how she'd recommitted everything to him. "I hoped that meant I could quit the campaign for prom queen," she said sadly. "But my friends aren't letting me off that easily." Now she actually laughed. "Although I'm sure I'll look totally ridiculous next week. Not only do I still not have a dress—I don't have a date either. So if you guys want a good laugh, I encourage you to come. Tickets are still on sale." Fortunately, this made them laugh now. She held up her hands in a hopeless gesture, then sat down.

"That took guts," Zoë whispered to her.

Megan just shrugged.

But as she drove Zoë home, she realized that Zoë was opening up to her more than ever. Not only had Zoë listened to the message tonight, but she seemed to be actually thinking about it. When Megan offered her a ride again next week, Zoë seemed glad to accept it.

"By the way," Zoë said as she was getting out of the car. "I'm still voting for you for prom queen, and I know a lot of others who are doing the same. You probably should try to find a dress." She grinned.

"Thanks." Megan frowned. "I think."

⚜

Megan couldn't believe how much more fun it was being in her skin on Monday. Even if she was the school joke—since thanks to some mouths from youth group, everyone knew that she was both dateless and dressless—she realized she didn't care. "God will take care of it," she assured her friends at lunch.

"God might expect you to help a little," Janelle pointed out.

"I'll do what I can." Megan shrugged. "I've actually been toying with the idea of asking Howard to be my escort."

Lishia groaned. "Okay, it's possible you're taking this humility thing a little too far."

"What does it matter? It's just a one-night deal. People make way too much of it." Megan considered telling them about Belinda's confession.

"That's true," Janelle agreed. "But since we're all trying to look nice, you could at least attempt to find a decent dress."

"And a date," Lishia added. "If that's not too much trouble."

"We were hoping to all go together," Chelsea reminded her. "The guys are arranging for a limo."

"I have an idea," Megan said suddenly. "Instead of going out to eat, what if I host a dinner at my house? I remember Belinda did that one year, and it seemed like they had a good time."

"It would save money," Chelsea said eagerly. "Nicholas was kind of complaining about how expensive everything was getting. I mean, in a nice way."

"It is expensive," Janelle agreed. "I like the idea of doing a dinner."

"We can all help," Lishia suggested.

"That's okay," Megan told them. "I'd actually like to take care of it myself." She smiled at them. "Kind of as a thank-you for you guys and the fundraiser. I still feel like I need to make that up to you."

Janelle nodded. "Hey, I'm good with that."

They all agreed.

"But that still doesn't provide you with a date," Lishia reminded her.

"Or a dress," Janelle pointed out.

"Well . . ." Megan thought hard. "I'll be working on it."

"Why don't we go shopping today?" Chelsea suggested. "Kate told me that some new gowns shipped this weekend. They should have them out on the rack tonight."

"A Best 4 Less dress?" Janelle looked skeptical.

"Hey, they have some great designer stuff sometimes," Chelsea said defensively.

"I know." Janelle nodded. "But don't let Amanda and Hallie hear about this or Megan will be the brunt of more of their jokes."

"I don't care," Megan assured her. "I'm already the brunt." She turned to Chelsea. "Thanks. I'd love your help with the dress." She looked at the others. "You guys want to come too?"

As it turned out, only she and Chelsea were free to go after school. "I have a pretty restricted budget," Megan admitted as they were going into the store. She didn't want to admit it was even more limited now that she'd offered to cater their meal for prom night. But really, she would rather put her money into a dinner for her friends than toward a formal gown she would only wear once and probably hate anyway.

❧

After close to two hours of trying on what felt like every dress in the store, Chelsea proclaimed the strapless fuchsia satin number a winner.

"Really?" Megan frowned at her image in the three-way mirror. Maybe her eyes were getting blurry or she was just sick, sick, sick of dresses, but she wasn't getting it. "This is the one?"

"Well, I'll admit it's a little big." Chelsea grasped the back of the dress and pulled it tighter. "But I called Kate while you were putting it on again, and she assured me that can be easily fixed, and you can tighten this sash."

Megan was about to protest. What if the seamstress took it in too much . . . or got it wrong . . . or didn't finish it on time? But then Megan realized she didn't really care. "Okay." She nodded with a little hesitation. "I'm getting it."

"Trust me, it's going to look great."

Megan smiled at her. "I do trust you." Really, why shouldn't she trust Chelsea? Not only did she have a good sense of style, but she'd been a rock through all of Megan's flakiness.

As Megan drove Chelsea home, she described Belinda's black strappy sandals. "Do you think those will work?"

"They sound perfect."

Megan sighed. "Thanks to you and your dad's store, I'm saving a bunch of money, Chelsea. Thanks."

Chelsea grinned. "It's not really my dad's store. He just works for them."

"Still, I appreciate it a lot."

"It's too bad Roxie had to see us shopping there tonight. She'll probably tell her friends."

"Probably." Megan just shrugged. "No big deal."

"You're not worried that Amanda or Hallie will tease you?"

"Oh, I'm sure Hallie will torture me accordingly," Megan admitted. "But, hey, I might just tell them. After all, they've both been asking me when and where I plan to get my dress. Why not just let the cat out of the bag myself?"

"Hallie does seem to have it in for you," Chelsea said.

"I suspect she's the one who started that rumor about how you're taking a girl as your date to prom."

"She turned a lot more vicious after Dayton forgave me. That really seemed to aggravate her."

"Well, she should be thankful she's still going to prom with him," Chelsea reminded her. "I have a feeling he'd rather go with you."

"Between you and me, he kinda hinted at that after he read my apology note. But I told him I'd rather just preserve our friendship." Megan smiled. "He still needs my writing help, so he's not pushing it."

⁂

By Wednesday morning, Megan's friends were getting seriously worried that she was going to be truly dateless for prom. "There's still Howard," she teased them as they helped her clear up the picked-over remnants of campaign goodies from her table. She was down to less than a dozen chocolate bars. Not that she cared. Mostly she'd be happy to see the last of them.

Janelle groaned. "That's getting less and less funny, Megan."

"I had a couple of suggestions," Lishia told them. "But Megan told me no way."

"Same here," Chelsea admitted.

"I just hate the idea of one of you guys cornering a date for me." Megan shrugged as she zipped her big pink bag. "I think I'd rather go alone."

"But that's so pathetic," Janelle told her.

"I don't know." Megan held her head high. "Maybe I'll send a message. That I am enough. I don't have to have a guy on my arm."

"But it's a dance," Lishia protested. "Who are you going to dance with if you don't have a guy?"

Megan feigned disappointment. "You won't share your dates?"

"Speaking of dates." Lishia nudged Megan's elbow. "There's your ex-date coming your way."

Megan looked up to see Jack approaching. His expression was hard to read, and so far, he hadn't even acknowledged her apology note. Not that she'd expected anything. Although it was surprising that Dayton, who she'd never considered the most thoughtful fellow, had seemed happy to forgive and forget. Of course, there was the tutoring thing to consider.

"Hey, Jack." She smiled as he stopped in front of her.

"Can we talk?" he asked quietly. "Privately?"

She nodded. "Sure." She tossed her friends a surprised glance, then followed Jack out to the courtyard. "What's up?" she asked as he paused by a column.

"Thanks for the note."

"Oh." She smiled. "No problem. I mean, you deserved more than just a letter, but at the time I didn't think you'd listen to me."

"You're probably right." He shoved his hands into his pockets. "Anyway, the musical is coming along pretty good."

"Oh, I'm glad to hear that."

"Clarisa is doing a good job with Golde."

Megan smiled. "I knew she would."

"Not as good as you would've."

She let out a sad sigh. "You know, Jack, I would've much rather continued with the musical than the prom campaign."

"I know. You explained that in the letter."

Now she didn't know what to say.

"Anyway, there's a rumor going around . . ."

She made a forced laugh. "You mean that I'm taking a girl to prom?" She rolled her eyes. "It's just a rumor."

"No, I mean that you don't have a date."

"Oh . . . that rumor." She pressed her lips together, wondering what he was getting at—after all, hadn't she heard he was taking Clarisa?

"So it's true?"

"Uh-huh." She tried to look nonchalant. She was not going to get her hopes up.

"Well, I got to thinking . . . Maybe I reacted a little strongly when you quit the musical. To be honest, it had been kind of a bad day. And rehearsal hadn't been too great. I think I was in a bad mood."

"You seemed pretty mad that day."

He nodded. "I was. But not completely at you."

"Oh." Was she imagining this? Or was he asking her to prom again?

"Anyway, if you don't have a date and you'd like to give me another shot . . ." He made a nervous smile.

"Are you asking me to prom, Jack?"

His brown eyes got bigger. "Yeah. You want to go with me?"

"I'd be honored to go with you."

"You forgive me for being such a jerk then?" He still looked a little worried.

"Of course."

He nodded. "And I forgive you."

She threw her arms around him. "It's a date."

After the hug ended, he gave her a sheepish smile. "Uh . . . we'll still have to use your car, okay?"

She explained about the limo and how she was fixing dinner at her house. He brightened. "Cool. I was getting a little worried about how expensive this was going to be."

"Don't worry, I'm a cheap date." She laughed.

twenty

By the end of the week, Megan was actually looking forward to prom, although she was probably most looking forward to having it all behind her by the weekend. Not that she wasn't glad to be going with Jack. Or relieved that her dress alterations had been successful. It was just so stressful knowing that she still had to stand up in front of everyone, smiling congenially as Amanda was crowned prom queen. Her one last form of public humiliation. Still, she was determined to hold her head high and then to have fun for the remainder of the evening.

It wasn't that she thought Amanda didn't deserve the crown. In fact, she planned to secretly vote for her, simply to help ensure that Hallie had less of a chance to win. Not that she thought Hallie had much of a chance anyway. But when Hallie showed up with a "salsa party" during the lunch hour—complete with Mexican music and virgin margaritas and some very enthusiastic fans, Megan wasn't so sure. She had to admit it was clever.

"Don't worry." Chelsea nodded to where the party seemed to be growing by the minute. "They're just there for the food."

Megan chuckled. "Can't blame them for that. Those mini tacos and chimichangas look pretty tempting."

"Speaking of food, what's on the menu tonight?" Lishia asked.

"Italian," Megan told them.

"Yum!" Janelle smacked her lips.

"My mom made her famous lasagna, and I'm making manicotti." Megan grinned. "The rest is a surprise, but trust me, I think it'll be good." The truth was, Megan had probably put as much thought and energy into tonight's dinner menu and preparations as she put into the prom. She didn't even care that dinner was taking so much of her time. If her friends enjoyed themselves at her house, she felt that the evening would be off to a decent start.

"You sure you don't need help with any of it?" Chelsea asked again.

"No." Megan firmly shook her head. "I want you guys to just come and have fun. Everything's under control."

Even so, she drove directly home from school that afternoon and went straight to work. Mom was letting her use the good china and crystal and silver. "Why not?" Mom had said. "We hardly ever use it anyway. What's it for if not to use?"

Still, Megan was careful as she set the table in the dining room. She'd put in the leaf to make it comfortable for eight. She'd also gotten fresh flowers and had candles ready to light, as well as a good selection of songs already on the MP3 player. She was just finishing up the green salad when Arianna and Olivia came home from their soccer game.

"Sorry we're late," Arianna told her.

"It's okay." Megan pointed to Olivia. "Did you remember to bring your server clothes?"

"Black pants and white shirt." Olivia said.

"And there are some tea towels to use as your aprons." Megan demonstrated how they could be lapped over a ribbon and tied to make them look like waiters in a fancy restaurant.

"This is fun," Olivia said with enthusiasm.

"And we still get paid, right?" Arianna said to Megan.

"Not just in pizza either," Megan assured them. "Although you're welcome to leftovers. There should be plenty." She glanced at the clock. "Mom should be home in a few minutes and—"

"You should go get ready." Arianna gently pushed her.

"Yeah," Olivia urged. "Don't you have to do your hair and stuff?"

Megan shrugged. "I'm not putting my hair up."

"You *have* to put it up," Arianna insisted. "It will look so elegant."

"I'm terrible at putting it up," Megan confessed. "I'll just wear it down."

"Let me call my mom," Olivia suddenly pulled out her phone. "She does hair. She used to be a hairdresser before I was born."

"That's right!" Arianna said eagerly. "She's great with hair."

Megan just held up her hands. "Whatever."

"Go get ready," Arianna said again. "You're burning daylight. And Mom won't want you around while she's playing head chef anyway."

"Okay." Megan took one last glance around the kitchen. Everything really did seem to be in good shape.

"Hurry!" Arianna urged her. "And don't forget to take a shower."

Megan chuckled as she went upstairs. Did Arianna honestly think she'd forget to take a shower? However, the truth was, she was not looking forward to getting dressed for the "big night." It was probably partially due to all the criticism she'd gotten from Belinda and partly because she still felt like such a fraud. But, she reminded herself, she had to do her best for her friends. They expected her to at least act like a candidate. She owed them that much.

After a quick shower, Megan slipped on the dress. Despite being taken in and fitting her figure much better, it was still comfortable. The zipper went up fairly easily. Plus the satiny fabric had just a little bit of give in it, so it was still comfortable to sit in. Not that she planned to sit all night, but it was nice knowing she wouldn't bust a seam if she bent over. She was just putting on her shoes—rather Belinda's shoes—when Olivia's mother knocked on her partially open door.

"Megan?" she called. "It's Ruth."

"Come in." Megan opened the door fully. She'd only met Olivia's mom a couple of times. "Sorry that Olivia dragged you into this."

"Nonsense. I think it'll be fun." Ruth set a small case on the dresser and pointed to the mirror. "Stand right here and I'll get straight to work. The girls said we don't have much time."

Megan glanced at the clock by her bed. "Yeah. My friends should be here in about fifteen minutes, and I still have—"

"Hold still." Ruth was vigorously brushing Megan's hair now. "How about a loose updo," she suggested. "With some up and some down?"

"Whatever you think is best."

Ruth looked surprised. "You seem awfully laid-back for a girl who's running for prom queen."

Megan laughed. "Well, I don't expect to win."

"That might be so, but how about I put in a few extra hairpins just in case someone sticks a crown up here, okay?"

"Whatever."

"Do you plan to wear a bit of makeup?" Ruth asked as she used a curling iron on some tendrils of hair.

"I put on lip gloss."

"Mind if I do a little touch-up?" Ruth smiled. "I learned makeup at cosmetology school too."

Megan frowned. "I just want to look natural—you know, like myself."

"I can respect that. I promise to keep it light. You'll look like yourself, only better. Okay?"

Megan wasn't so sure. But as she looked more closely at her hair, which actually looked great, her confidence grew. "Okay. If you think so."

Ruth turned Megan away from the mirror now. "Just relax, honey."

Megan took in a deep breath, and as Ruth quietly worked, she prayed that she wouldn't come out looking like a drag queen.

"Oh, Megan," Mom gushed as she came into the room. "You look gorgeous!"

"Really?" Megan blinked.

"Careful of the mascara," Ruth warned.

"Really beautiful." Mom nodded eagerly, keeping her hands behind her back.

"How's dinner?" Megan asked nervously. "Did you put the bread in to warm and—"

"Everything's under control. Remember our agreement. You do the first part and let me do the rest. Right?"

Megan nodded. "Right."

Mom pulled out her jewelry box and opened it. "I just wanted to see if there's something in here you'd like to wear tonight, sweetie."

"Really?" Megan stared down into the box. Mom actually had some pretty nice pieces of jewelry. Dad had been generous when they'd been together.

"Why not?" Mom pulled out a pendant and held it up. "The big stone is just a garnet, but the small stones are diamonds."

"That's nice with the dress," Ruth observed.

"Or the pearls." Mom held up a strand. "Or are they too matronly?"

"They're all pretty," Megan declared. "How can I decide?"

They watched as she tried on various pieces and combinations and finally settled on the garnet pendant, diamond stud earrings, and a garnet cocktail ring.

"How's that?" Mom asked as Megan took one last look at her reflection.

"I feel like a princess," Megan admitted.

"Well, here's to you being crowned queen," Ruth said as she closed her case.

Megan was just thanking both of them when the doorbell rang.

"That's probably your guests," Mom said. "I told the girls to serve appetizers and champagne in the living room."

"Champagne?" Ruth looked alarmed.

"Sparkling cider," Mom explained.

Megan thanked them both again, then hurried down to greet her friends. Of course, they all looked gorgeous—even the guys. "You look fantastic," Jack told her as he helped her with a wrist corsage. It was tiny dark pink roses tied with a silver ribbon.

"Thank you." She held up her wrist. "This is beautiful."

"Not as beautiful as you," he said quietly.

She beamed at him. This was so much more than she'd expected. "Thanks. You look great too."

"Everyone looks so glamorous," she told the others as she led them to the living room. "Very Hollywood."

"All ready for the red carpet," Lishia said happily.

"Look at this." Chelsea picked up one of the carefully made appetizers, holding it up for the others to see. "Very uptown, Megan." She winked. "By the way, you look gorgeous too."

Everyone seemed to relax as they munched on the appetizers, and by the time dinner was ready, the eight of them were having so much fun that one of the guys suggested they just skip the prom altogether.

"We can't do that," Chelsea said as they headed into the dining room. "We have to see Megan get crowned tonight."

Megan laughed. "Don't hold your breath on that."

"You have a chance," Lishia insisted as they sat down.

"Let's not be delusional." Megan shook her head as she unfolded her cloth napkin. "But at least I finished the race."

"Here's to finishing," Jack held up his sparkling cider in a toast.

The rest of them followed his lead. After that toast ended, Megan decided to make another. "Here's to my good friends," she said happily. "The one thing I learned through my silly pursuit of the crown is that nothing matters more than my friends. I would rather have you guys than a crown of real gold and diamonds—and that's the truth."

"Well, just in case," Janelle warned, "I hope you have an acceptance speech planned."

Megan rolled her eyes. "Yeah, sure, Janelle."

Arianna and Olivia began to serve dinner, and thankfully, the conversation switched over to food and other things. Megan really just wanted to forget that before the evening was over, she would have to stand on the stage and watch Amanda be crowned. It wasn't that she didn't want to watch Amanda being crowned. It was simply that she wished, truly wished, she could be watching it from the dance floor with her friends. But at least it would be over tonight.

She looked around the table at her friends and smiled. She remembered how Belinda had said that prom night was her happiest high school memory. At the time, Megan had assumed it was because of winning the crown, and perhaps it was like that for Belinda. But Megan thought this moment—sharing a meal with her friends, laughing and enjoying each other—might end up being one of her happiest moments.

Finally the meal came to an end and Chelsea insisted that it was time to get to the actual prom. "We can't have our prom queen candidate showing up late," she said as she helped herd everyone toward the door.

Megan simply had to bite her tongue. She had no illusions about how this was going to go down. But she would play along and let her friends enjoy this. The ride in the limo was fun, rocking out to an old Beatles CD that the driver cranked up for them. But before they got there, Nicholas got very quiet and serious as he read a message on his iPhone. "Oh no," he said. "This is bad."

"What is it?" Chelsea asked him.

"Well, I hate to be a downer tonight . . ."

"Tell us," Chelsea demanded.

"Yes," Megan urged. "Please do."

"I don't want to spoil your big night, Megan."

She firmly shook her head. "It is not *my* big night. It's *everyone's* big night. Now, please, tell us what's wrong."

"The text is from Pastor Raymond, and it's about Bethany Bridgewater."

"What happened?" Janelle asked.

"She's been having some tests at the hospital. They thought she had a bone infection, but turns out it's some kind of cancer," Nicholas said solemnly.

"Oh, poor Bethany," Lishia said.

"Oh no." Megan felt a rush of sadness.

"Will she still be at prom?" Janelle asked. "I know she and Michael were planning on going."

"The text says she's still coming," Nicholas told them. "In a wheelchair. She's not supposed to put any weight on the leg."

"Let's pray for her," Megan said suddenly. "Let's ask God to give her a special night despite everything. And let's ask him to heal her too."

So right there in the limo, all eight of them bowed their heads and prayed for Bethany Bridgewater. And then they were at the prom.

"I have a good feeling about Bethany," Lishia said as they started getting out of the limo. "Like she's going to beat this."

"Me too," Megan told her. "But we'll have to keep praying for her." Suddenly she felt nervous as she remembered what this night was all about. Yet at the same time, she felt foolish for ever having been so obsessed with something so superficial. Especially in light of what Bethany was experiencing.

"Just relax," Jack whispered in her ear as he helped her out of the limo.

"Is it that obvious?" she asked.

He made a concerned smile. "You seem like you're tensing up."

"I just want to get the whole crowning biz over with," she said quietly. "I know Amanda's going to win. I just want to get beyond it and spend time with you and my friends."

"What if you *do* win?" He linked arms with her.

She made a tolerant smile. "That's pretty much impossible now."

"Everyone in the musical sounded like they were voting for you," he told her as they went inside.

She blinked in surprise. "Seriously?"

He nodded. "You're like the drama representative."

"Even so, that's a small percentage of students." Catching a heel on something, she tightened her hold on his arm. "Still, it's sweet."

They settled in at a table, and soon the couples took to the dance floor. Megan thought that if she could just forget she still had to get on that stage with the other girls, she could be just fine. As more people entered the room, she kept a watch out for Bethany and Michael. It would be hard to miss a wheelchair. Finally, just as the principal was making her way to the stage, Megan saw Michael pushing Bethany into prom in a wheelchair, with several of their friends trailing happily behind them. It was a relief to see their smiles.

But now all attention was on Mrs. Morgan as she made a little speech and then called the prom queen candidates up to the stage, giving them each a short introduction. Megan knew from the last prom committee meeting that the candidates were expected to be escorted to the stage by their dates, and then the guys would line up off to one side. She'd already explained this to Jack.

"And this, ladies and gentleman"—Mrs. Morgan waved an envelope with a big gold seal on the back—"holds the final results. Are you ready to crown this year's queen?"

Some clapping and whoops came from the onlookers. Feeling silly and conspicuous, Megan just waited, biding her time.

"This year's prom queen is *Megan Bernard*."

Megan frowned at Mrs. Morgan, certain that she'd read the card wrong. Or else Megan had heard her wrong.

"It's *you*." Hallie gave Megan a sharp nudge.

"But—"

"Go on," Amanda told her.

"But it can't—"

"Megan Bernard," Mrs. Morgan said happily, "come and get your crown."

Megan's knees felt wobbly, and her stomach was turning upside down. Not only that, but it felt as if her shoes were glued to the stage. Like a bad dream.

"Come on, Megan." Jack linked his arm in hers. "Let's go get your crown."

To her relief, he walked her over to where Mrs. Morgan was waiting with the crown. But when he tried to step away, as Mrs. Morgan secured the crown to her head, Megan held tight. She knew that without him, she would probably fall over. She was presented with a bouquet of roses.

"Okay, Megan, go ahead." Mrs. Morgan pointed to the microphone. "Speech time."

Megan looked at her with frightened eyes, wishing this nightmare would end.

"Your royal subjects are waiting." Mrs. Morgan gave her a worried look.

"Just talk to your friends," Jack whispered.

As she stepped to the mic, Megan shot up a quick "help me" prayer. "Thank you all so much," she began slowly. "I guess you can see how shocked I am to have won this honor. I honestly didn't think I'd win. I didn't even prepare a speech." She took in a fast breath. "The only reason I'm up here is because you guys believed in me." She smiled now. "And I think the reason you believed in me is because I'm just a regular girl. Like most of you. So me winning this crown is like we all won it. Right?" Several people clapped at this.

"This prom is for everyone—to have fun and enjoy the last big event before graduation. I hope you're all doing that.

Are you?" More clapping erupted. "So I'll keep this short. But first I want to thank my really good friends for standing by me—even when I wasn't much fun to be around. I also want to thank God for reminding me to keep my feet on the ground. I learned a lot while campaigning for prom queen." She paused to consider what she wanted to say.

"The most important thing I've learned—I think I'm actually realizing it right this moment—is that the true purpose of royalty is to care for its subjects. To put your subjects' needs above your own." Megan laughed. "Not that you're really my subjects. But I think a good queen would realize that she's really nothing more than a servant to her people. Not someone who should be waited on and treated in a special way. Because I know everyone out there is more important than I am. So why am I still talking?" She laughed. "I just hope you all have a really fantastic and memorable evening!" She held up her bouquet like a scepter. "And God bless!"

The music began to play again, and following tradition, Megan and Jack began to dance, followed by the rest of the court. But as soon as the dance ended, Megan and Jack went over to rejoin their friends, where more hugs and congratulations were shared.

"Look," Lishia said suddenly, nodding over to the dance floor.

Megan turned to see that Michael had parked Bethany's wheelchair on the side of the dance floor and was now lifting the petite girl up into his arms. "Oh my!" Megan watched as he carried Bethany onto the floor, holding her securely as they danced to an especially romantic song. The other girls let out little oohs and aahs as they watched. Megan removed the crown from her head.

"What are you doing?" Janelle demanded.

"This crown belongs to all of us," Megan told them. "I want everyone to have a chance to wear it, and I think Bethany deserves it next."

As the song ended, Megan went over and placed the crown on Bethany's head. "We're going to take turns wearing it."

"But you can't do—"

"I'm the queen, am I not?" Megan asked her.

"Yes . . . well . . ."

"And I hereby declare that we are all queens tonight! And any girl here—starting with you and my good friends— anyone who wants to wear the crown is welcome to a turn." She gave her head a shake, relieved to be free from the weight of the crown. "Now let's all make this a night to remember!"

A Note from the Author

Art Imitating Life

You may not realize that Bethany Bridgewater is a real girl and not a fictional character. Bethany came into my life through the Make-A-Wish Foundation in July 2012, after Bethany expressed her wish to write a book with me. Well, I'm a fast writer, but it would be impossible to write an entire book in just one day. Since I was in the final edit stages of this book, I decided to turn a real scene out of Bethany's life into a scene in *The Prom Queen*. Fact meets fiction!

Bethany really did participate in show choir. She did suffer leg pains after a performance shortly before her own prom.

And she was diagnosed with a form of cancer called Ewing's sarcoma. But because she so wanted to attend prom, her doctors delayed her much-needed chemo treatment and surgery a couple of days so that she and her date could go to prom. Much like it's written in this book, he did pick Bethany up and carry her to the dance floor, turning that prom into a night that Bethany will never forget. Thanks to excellent medical treatment and God's miraculous mystery, Bethany is a rare positive statistic and on her way to recovery.

Because Bethany wants to be a writer, I'll be helping her to craft a memoir about her journey through cancer. Right now we're calling it *Swallowing the Red Devil*, but as with many things in life, titles change. As the memoir gets closer to publication, I'll try to keep you updated on my website.

For more information about the Make-A-Wish Foundation, go to www.wish.org.

Melody Carlson is the award-winning author of over two hundred books, including *The Jerk Magnet*, *The Best Friend*, *Never Been Kissed*, *Double Take*, and the Diary of a Teenage Girl series. Melody recently received a Romantic Times Career Achievement Award in the inspirational market for her books. She and her husband live in central Oregon. For more information about Melody, visit her website at www.melodycarlson.com.

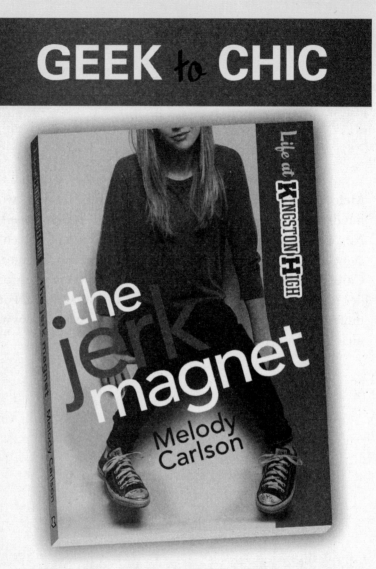

Meet Melody at
MelodyCarlson.com

....

- Enter a contest for a signed book
- Read her monthly newsletter
- Find a special page for book clubs
- Discover More Books by Melody

Become a fan on Facebook
Melody Carlson Books

Aster Flynn Wants a Life of Her Own . . .

But will her family get in her way?

New School = New Chance
for That First Kiss

Just when it seems Elise is on top of the world, everything comes crashing down. Could one bad choice derail her future?